RICHARD SCARSBROOK

THE TROUPERS

Cormorant Books

This is a first edition.

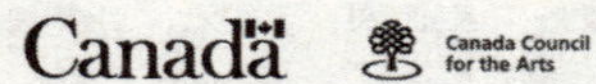
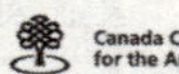
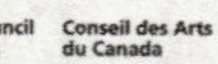

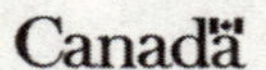

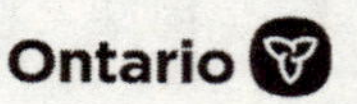

We acknowledge financial support for our publishing activities: the Government of Canada through the Canada Book Fund and The Canada Council for the Arts; the Government of Ontario, through the Ontario Arts Council, Ontario Creates, and the Ontario Book Publishing Tax Credit. We acknowledge additional funding provided by the Government of Ontario and the Ontario Arts Council to address the adverse effects of the novel coronavirus pandemic.

LIBRARY AND ARCHIVES CATALOGUING IN PUBLICATION

Title: The Troupers / Richard Scarsbrook.
Names: Scarsbrook, Richard, author.
Identifiers: Canadiana (print) 20210212667 | Canadiana (ebook) 20210212675 | ISBN 9781770866300 (softcover) | ISBN 9781770866317 (HTML)
Classification: LCC PS8587.C396 T76 2021 | DDC C813/.54—dc23

United States Library of Congress Control Number: 2021938487

Cover design: Angel Guerra / Archetype
Interior text design: Tannice Goddard, tannicegdesigns.ca
Printer: Friesens
Printed and bound in Canada.
Manufactured by Friesens in Altona, Manitoba in August, 2021.

CORMORANT BOOKS INC.
260 SPADINA AVENUE, SUITE 502, TORONTO, ON, M5T 2E4
www.cormorantbooks.com

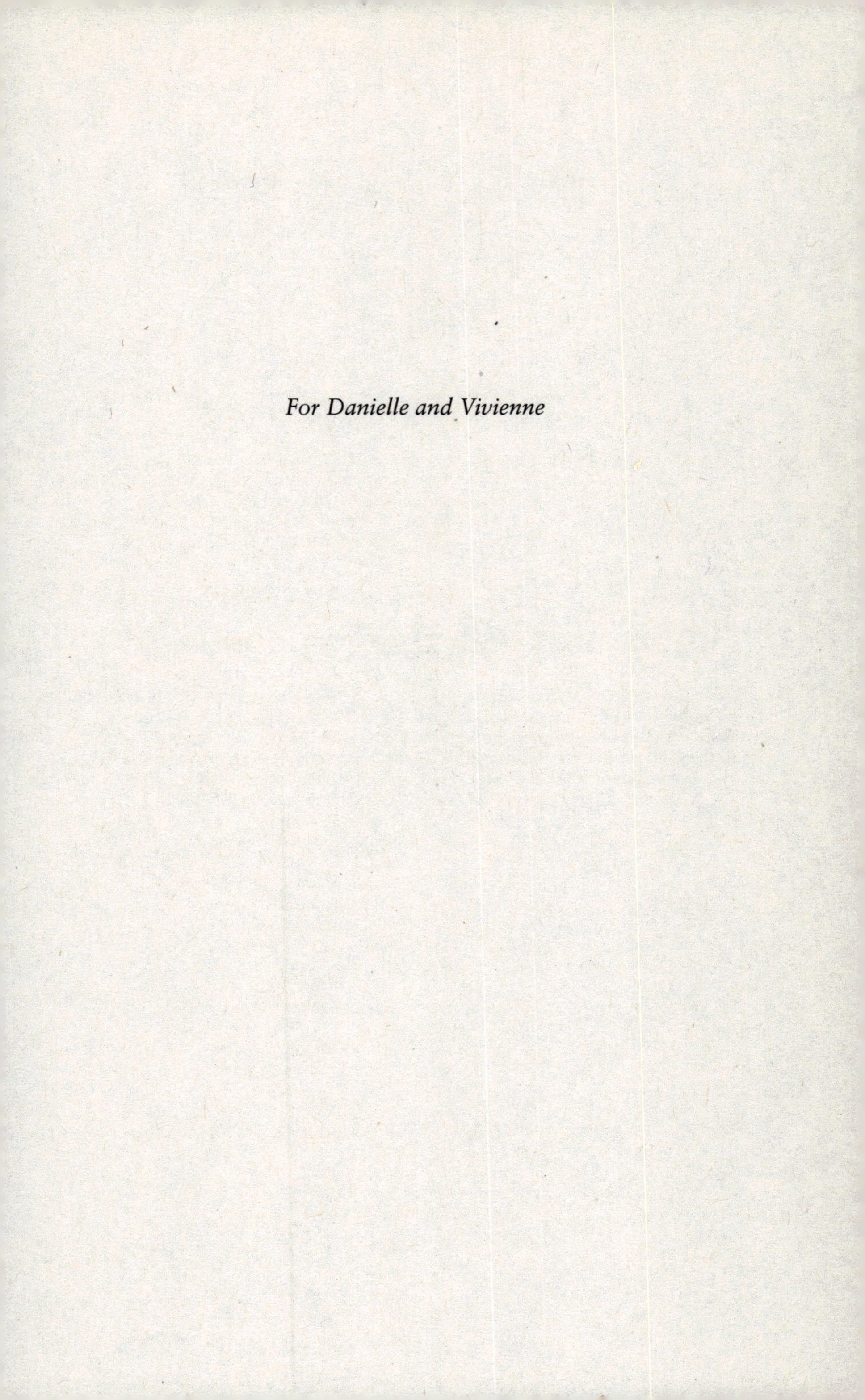

For Danielle and Vivienne

Scene 1:

The Nightmare Variations

(Or: Late-Night Triple Feature)

THERE ARE THREE VARIATIONS of the dream.

In the first version, I am driving the car. Everything is vivid, vintage Technicolor, all primary and secondary tones, as if coloured with a pack of grade-school crayons. The sky is Pacific Blue, and the paper-white clouds overhead are traced in Sunset Orange. The car is Basic Black.

I am as I was when I was eight years old, and Marigold is also the eight-year-old version of herself. Her hair is in pigtails, and she is wearing her angel costume with the gold satin wings.

Our mother is as she was before her exile, calmly self-confident, regally poised, and naturally beautiful.

We are driving with the top down, the wind rushing around us in Periwinkle Blue streaks, laughing together, our voices slightly out of sync, half-harmonizing like three different versions of the same song, "HA HA HA."

And then I am plucked from the car by the back of my shirt collar, gripped by what feels like the thumb and index finger of a supernaturally huge yet invisible hand. My feet dangle uselessly above the pavement as the car races forward without me, toward a curve in the Slate Grey road, and then it plunges over the ledge and down into the steep river gorge.

The invisible hand lifts me up higher so I can see over the cliff, its rough walls jagged lines of Eggplant Purple and Shadow Brown, as if scribbled by an angry toddler. Way down below, the banks of the river are thick scratches of Burnt Sienna edged with Pine Green. The deep, roaring water is a violent scrawl of Midnight Blue.

Then the invisible hand lowers me into the gorge so I can witness the car smashing down, collapsing upon itself like a toy accordion, its nose burrowing into the Tumbleweed Tan earth. My mother and my sister are thrown free, and they shatter into billions of tiny, complicated jigsaw puzzle pieces.

Frantically, I try to gather their fragments and put them back together, but I've only managed to join together two pieces of Marigold — and none of our mother — before the river overspills its banks and sweeps the rest of their pieces into its rushing, churning current.

I try to run into the water, but the phantom hand holds me back, and all I can do is watch as their puzzle fragments disappear under a thick layer of Midnight Blue.

IN THE SECOND VARIATION of the dream, everything appears in vivid black and white, with dramatic lighting and crisp-edged shadows, like a 1940s Hollywood movie directed by Michael Curtiz.

In this version of the dream, I'm flying.

I soar through the grainy, silver-toned air as if I'm swimming atop the calm surface of the warm, buoyant Dead Sea. Then I realize that there are Rolls-Royce Merlin fighter plane engines built into the palms of my hands and the soles of my feet, so I propel myself through the sky at a ludicrous rate of speed.

From high up above, I see teenaged Marigold behind the wheel of the Renault Floride, with our mother, as we last knew her, in the passenger seat. They are racing toward that fatal curve in the road, laughing together, oblivious to the danger, "HA HA HA."

I blast through the air to catch up with them, accompanied by the announcer's voice from a 1940s radio serial: "Faster than a speeding bullet ... it's a bird ... it's a plane ... it's *Superman*!" I execute a high-speed dive toward the zooming car, accompanied by the screaming sound of a diving warplane, like I'm Gregory Peck in *Twelve O'Clock High*.

Then I realize with a start that this is really the sound of Wile E. Coyote falling to what should be his death in a Road Runner cartoon. I slam into a repelling force like a sheet of unbreakable glass, and I lie flattened upon it in midair, motionless, unable to do anything but watch the Floride plummet over the cliff with Marigold and our mother inside.

The invisible barrier in the sky holds me against it like the gravity of a hundred Earths. My face is plastered against its transparent surface. It holds my eyelids open. It forces me to witness everything that happens next.

Echoing, cackling laughter surrounds me, like Vincent Price in *House of Wax*, as Marigold and our mother are swallowed by the river.

MY OTHER SISTERS HAVE, at different times, suggested that I really should see a psychiatrist to help me sort all of this out, but honestly, I don't think it's necessary; I've read all of the relevant books.

In *The Interpretation of Dreams*, Sigmund Freud writes, "Dreams are the royal road to the unconscious" and "They completely satisfy wishes excited during the day which remain unrealized. They are simply and undisguisedly realizations of wishes."

Carl Jung, in *The Meaning of Psychology for Modern Man*, states, "The dream is a little hidden door in the innermost and most secret recesses of the soul" and "Dreams are impartial, spontaneous products of the unconscious psyche, outside the control of the will. They are pure nature; they show us the unvarnished, natural truth."

Henri-Frédéric Amiel says, "The dream is the reflection of the waves of the unconscious life in the floor of the imagination." In my case, though, I suppose it's more like the effect of a spotlight aimed at another actor, whose shadow darkens the floorboards of the stage upon which I am about to step out and perform ... or something like that.

And I know I shouldn't mislead myself by calling them dreams. They are nightmares.

THE THIRD VERSION OF the nightmare is probably the closest approximation of what may have actually happened that night; it bears the most resemblance to what the police officer told me on the veranda, anyway.

In the muted, impressionistic tones of a faded 1970s-era documentary film, our mother is already dead as the swollen river sweeps her body away from the wreckage.

But Marigold is still alive.

Her head bobs above the surface of the angry water, which hisses and bubbles like a cauldron about to boil over. Her backpack, with its sewn-on golden angel wings, is dragging her under, and she thrashes and twists to free herself from it.

I am frozen at the top of the cliff as she screams out to me, "Where are you, Errol? Why aren't you here?"

Her backpack washes up onshore, and when I look back at the roaring water, Marigold has disappeared.

And this is where I am when, in the space outside the nightmare, the phone rings.

THE TV FLICKERS AT the foot of the bed. The remote is still in my hand.

"And now," the announcer's voice intones, "the conclusion to the Classic Movie Channel's Late-Night Triple Feature."

I push the power button, and the room goes dark.

Atop the dresser beside my bed, the phone rings again. I see my sister Olivia's name on the glowing call display screen.

As I grip the phone and push the talk button, I feel that supernaturally huge invisible hand pressing down on me, and in the pause before Olivia speaks, I think I know why she's calling: Marigold's body has been found at last, and I can finally, finally allow myself to let her go.

But it turns out that Olivia is calling for another reason.

Scene 2:

The Reunion Show

(Or: Meet the Cast!)

THE TAXI I'M RIDING in crawls up the Niagara Parkway behind a parade of tour buses, minivans, and SUVs filled with tourists whose faces are pressed up against the windows to get a glimpse of the Falls as they pass. There is a faint rainbow arching through the mist today, so the cameras on their phones and tablets will be working overtime, taking similar shots of the flash from their device reflecting back from the glass of their vehicle's window.

We inch our way toward Clifton Hill, past the old strip motels whose yellowed marquees brag in all caps about FREE WI-FI and BUFFET BREAKFAST and IN-SUITE HEART-SHAPED HOT TUBS, past the towering luxury hotels, past the wax museum, past the phony stucco-plastered Gothic towers of the haunted house, past the fallen-sideways imitation of the Empire State Building with the flaking purple statue of King Kong hanging from its tower.

And now I finally see it again, after so many years: the Art Deco–retrofitted neo-Romanesque façade of the theatre where my sisters and I spent so much of our lives. Echoing the famous sign at Radio City Music Hall in New York City, it announces itself in bold, red neon letters, framed in glowing blue:

THE

TROUPER-ROYALE
ORPHEUM-GALAXIE

THEATRE

And upon its backlit movie theatre–style marquee, the following bold promise is made:

THE JEWEL IN THE
ENTERTAINMENT CROWN OF
NIAGARA FALLS
FOR 100 YEARS!
1918–2018

The traffic on Clifton Hill has come to a standstill, so I pay my fare, hop out of the taxi, and weave through the ambling, wide-eyed crowds of tourists. When I reach the grand façade of the Orpheum-Galaxie, I slip through the narrow alleyway between it and the funhouse next door.

A prickly feeling overtakes me, like spiders crawling up the back of my neck, and I look back. A slender, hooded figure, dressed from head to toe in black, is watching me from the end of the alley.

When I blink, the dark figure is gone. Just a shadow. Just my imagination.

I take a deep breath and keep going.

At the back of the theatre, in the centre of the windowless, grime-and-smoke-blackened brick wall, is a single, rust-speckled metal door, with these words stencilled upon it in black spray paint:

NO PUBLIC ENTRANCE
CAST MEMBERS ONLY

As I reach for the door handle, I hesitate. Even after all this time, I am still not ready to face him.

I close my eyes and hold my breath, and I hear Marigold's gentle voice whispering, "You can't go forward until you go back."

Imaginary Marigold is right, of course, so I open my eyes and exhale. Then I turn the handle, push open the door, and make my way through the darkened corridor that leads backstage.

NORMALLY, A PERFORMER EXPOSING their face to the audience before a show would be prohibited by our father, but since he isn't the director of this afternoon's performance, I'm breaking the rule. No one in the audience will be able to see me, anyway, since the spotlights are turned off and it is dark onstage. I peek out through the thin slit between the curtain's edge and the stage right wall to take a look.

It's a full house out there. Packed to the rafters. Standing room only. A sold-out show.

When my sisters and I all left this theatre on the day of our collective eighteenth birthday, each of us vowed that we would never return, that the Fabulous Trouper Quintuplets would never again perform upon this stage. But here we are once more: four out of five of us, anyway.

And that's why every single seat in the auditorium is filled. We are the reason that the aisles and doorways are jammed with bodies. None of them want to miss this performance; it's the first time in over twenty years that the surviving members of the Trouper Family have been onstage together, and this matinee will be our one and only appearance.

Although the audience that fills the Orpheum-Galaxie is trying to respect the solemnity of this occasion, to restrain their voices to reverent whispers, I can hear the excited anticipation in the muffled rumble that seeps through the gilt-edged crimson curtain.

Will there be controversy? Unforeseen plot twists? Emotional outbursts? Drama? Violence? Betrayal? It's the Troupers, after all.

Positioned at centre stage, behind the closed curtain, is the man they have all come to see: the Lion of the Stage and Screen. Winner of a Dora and a Genie. Companion of the Order of Thespians, with a Star on their Walk of Fame.

Our Director. Our Producer. Our Manager.

Our father.

The One and Only John Lionel Trouper.

His eyes are closed and his facial features are at rest, a backstage ritual observed throughout his entire illustrious career: Keep it all in reserve. Don't come alive until you feel the heat of the spotlight on your face, the swish of the curtain opening, or the director calling, "Action." Save it for the show.

John Lionel has always insisted on working only with Madeline "Mademoiselle" Murdoch as his makeup artist, ever since those first wrinkles began working their way outward from the corners of his eyes, and her makeup brush sorcery made it possible for the aging thespian to play characters that were ten or sometimes even twenty years younger than the man himself. Mademoiselle has come out of retirement to touch up her favourite client one last time, and she has done a fabulous job on him, as always, brushing black into his grey hair, filling in the valleys that subdivide his forehead, trowelling over the deep tributaries that reach out from the corners of his eyes, erasing with flesh-toned powder the blue veins that cobweb his temples.

Our father still has the dashing, dignified good looks of the greying Cary Grant in *Charade* with Audrey Hepburn (although his physique has become more reminiscent of Sydney Greenstreet in *The Maltese Falcon*). When the curtain opens, more than one member of the audience will whisper, "My, doesn't he look wonderful?" (with the addendum "for a man his age" remaining implied). He looks wise yet playful, weathered yet virile, accomplished yet adventurous; as it always is with great stage veterans, it is difficult to tell where the actor ends and the character begins (and vice versa).

He is costumed in a generously cut navy blue double-breasted suit, as befits a man of his prominence; his once-athletic figure has rounded out into a shape that he himself would describe as "prosperous." Each polished brass button on his suit jacket is embossed with a pseudo-English coat of arms. The golden links that glint upon his French cuffs are shaped like the comedy and drama masks. A huge ring encircles the middle finger of his left hand, embossed with a knight's helmet and surrounded by little diamonds. And, of course, the most important detail, his character's trademark: the golden cravat tucked perfectly into his high white collar.

When the curtain opens, every spotlight in the house will blaze upon him, and his accoutrements will glimmer like stars against the black velvet backdrop.

He isn't the director this time, but every other element of this production has been under his control from the beginning:

Written by .... **John Lionel Trouper**
Produced by.. **John Lionel Trouper**
Casting by.. **John Lionel Trouper**
Starring.. **John Lionel Trouper**

With this final show, his legacy will be complete. Now it is the responsibility of the cast to stick to the script and perform our assigned roles. The Great John Lionel Trouper is depending on us!

Ladies and gentlemen and children of all ages, introducing the supporting cast of this afternoon's most anticipated performance:

Playing the Beautiful, Dramatic, Emotional Daughter .... **Joan Trouper**

My sister Joan was the firstborn of the Trouper Quintuplets, and she is usually the scene-stealer in any production. She was named by our father after Joan Crawford, and she is the one Trouper Quintuplet whose name completely suits her; the feisty, vainglorious, dramatic spirit of Joan Crawford fills and animates her namesake, never to be exorcised.

Joan is positioned just one half-step stage left of our father, with her hands clasped against her chest. Tears are already welling in her eyes, to be released on cue the moment the curtain swings. This is the role that Joan was born to play.

There will potentially be producers, directors, and casting agents in the audience today, and if Joan plays her part well in the Troupers' reunion performance, maybe she can remind them of the gifted, larger-than-life young actress she once was. Perhaps she will earn comparisons to her namesake's performance in *Humoresque*, or perhaps Vivien Leigh in *Gone with the Wind*. Regardless, all eyes and every camera in the room will zoom in on her, if not because of the magnetic pull of her dark, tear-glistening eyes, then because she is dressed in an outfit much like the one worn by Crawford in *Grand Hotel*, which suits the tone of the production but also displays just enough of her proudly maintained physique. Either way, Joan Trouper will accept and absorb any approval and applause that is cast her way.

Playing the Angry, Displaced, Misunderstood Daughter .... **Violet Trouper**

Violet, the second-born Trouper Quint, was named by our mother; our father wanted to name all of his offspring after famous Golden Age actors, but our mother, Lily, wanted to name her girls after flowers, and her opinion was supported for perhaps the first and only time by our paternal grandmother, Chrysanthemum. So, after much debate, a compromise was reached, and two of the Trouper Quintuplets are named after flowers, and three are named after actors (our father won the coin toss for the final choice).

As a child, spunky, sporty, defiant Violet despised her name, but as an adult she has grown to appreciate it, if only because it sounds like "Violent," and in the punk rock business, anger and aggression sell a lot of albums, T-shirts, and concert tickets. In direct contrast to Joan's 1940s *femme fatale* costume, Violet's current outfit consists of a plain black tank top beneath a denim vest randomly decorated with buttons and patches with the names of punk, metal, and hardcore bands like Pissoff Anarchy, Skullcrusher, and The Exploiters. Her legs are encased in shredded, bleach-spattered jeans and a pair of tall, black motorcycle boots festooned with chrome-plated buckles, skull-shaped studs, and chains styled to look like barbed wire.

Violet stands upstage in the shadow cast by Joan. Her twitching, wiry arms are crushed against her chest, and her lips are pursed tightly as she glares into the waves of Joan's thick brown hair, as if she longs to ram the gel-hardened points of her spiked, dyed-even-blonder hair through the back of Joan's skull.

I try to send Violet a reassuring glance from across the stage, but she is so focused on incinerating Joan by radiating ultraviolet hatred through her eyes that she doesn't see me or anyone else. I realize now that I've unconsciously shuffled backward, as far from Violet and Joan as is geometrically possible upon this stage; I've learned to never stand too close to them when they're at odds with each other, which is pretty much all the time. Olivia possesses this wisdom, too, which is why she is also standing over here right now, across the stage next to me, as far as possible from Violet and Joan.

Playing the Practical, Studious, ... **Olivia Trouper**
Responsible Daughter

Of all of the Fabulous Trouper Quintuplets, it is Olivia who has changed the most since the last time we were onstage together, especially her appearance — and it is appearances that will matter most to our audience today. She's had her hair cut into a businesslike bob, and she's costumed in one of the conservative, earth-toned, hemmed-below-the-knee skirt suits that she wears every weekday as a development executive at AMUSEMENT ELEVEN™, the "Largest Provider of Entertainment Content in the World."

Olivia looks at me over the rims of her fashionable-but-practical bifocal glasses and whispers, "I hope Joan and Violet can hold it together."

I whisper back to her, "Thanks for taking care of all the last-minute details, Olivia."

"My pleasure," she says without pleasure. Then she glances across the stage at Joan and Violet and sighs. "You know what I was thinking about this morning? I was thinking about how much my name still bugs me. What a weird thing for me to be thinking about, on today of all days. But it still annoys me. Every day it reminds me that, no matter what I do, I'm always the Olivia de Havilland character in this cast."

It's true. She always is.

I try to think of something to say that will make her feel better, so I offer, "Hey, at least Olivia de Havilland is still alive. She celebrated her hundredth birthday two years ago."

"So I get to be old?" Olivia says. "Great. I've got that to look forward to."

I shrug. "At least you'll be able to afford it. I've got enough savings to last me until I'm ... well, until next month's rent is due."

She rolls her eyes. "Money isn't everything, Errol."

How easy it is for people with money to say things like that.

Olivia crosses her arms and glares into the shadows of the stage right curtains, signalling that our conversation is over for now.

As I glance around the darkened stage at my sisters, none of them looking at me nor at one another, something occurs to me: even as twenty-first-century adults, we are all still more or less just playing the same stock characters, performing the same roles that our father cast us in as children.

Except for Marigold, of course.

Something compels me to peek out once again through the thin slit in the curtains, and as the house lights dim and the noise of the crowd fades to a hum, in the mass of shadowy faces I suddenly see her, as if a spotlight has suddenly illuminated her face.

It's Marigold.

She's out there.

My heart races. I knew it!

I've always known it.

Marigold is alive.

Playing the Sweet, Kind, Empathetic Daughter .... **Marigold Trouper**

I want to call out to her, I want to break through the curtain, to rush through the audience, up the aisle, and across the row, to embrace her and never let her go again …

But then I blink, and I blink again, and her doppelgänger, or her phantom, or whatever I think I just saw, vanishes as the auditorium goes dark.

As I shuffle back to my opening position onstage, Olivia whispers, "You okay? You look like you just saw a ghost."

Before I can respond, the funeral director says from just offstage, "Everyone ready?" and then reaches up for the rope that will part the curtains and reveal us all to the buzzing capacity crowd out there.

I glance over at our father, and I straighten myself and shake off any evidence of emotion from my face and body. When the moment arrives, I will be performing my role in the style of Buster Keaton, the Great Stone Face. I'll be stoic, deadpan, unflappable … and silent.

I was the last born of the Fabulous Trouper Quintuplets, but I am also the only son. In another time, in another culture, in another family, this would probably have earned me second billing after my illustrious father, but not in this troupe, and especially not in this production.

Since the day I was born, I've never lived up to our father's expectations for any role he's cast me in, so no one is going to see any "acting" from me today. I will emphasize no lines, I will make no memorable gestures, I will express no emotions. I will leave all the performing to John Lionel Trouper's beloved daughters. They can have all of the applause, too.

Playing the Son Who Should Have Been a Daughter .... **Errol Trouper**

Yes, our father named me after that swashbuckling ladies' man, Errol Flynn — such wishful thinking!

As the gilt-edged velvet curtain creeps open, there is a surge in the rumble of voices, like a wave rolling in from the sea of spectators toward the sand-coloured hardwood beach of the stage. The wave crashes in a foaming "Shhhhhhhhhhh!" and then recedes, replaced by the silence of hundreds holding their breath.

Scene 3:

The Curtain Call

(Or: Always Save It for the Show)

AS THE LIGHTS BLAZE overhead, the director says, "Action!"; for the first time ever, this word does not activate John Lionel Trouper. He does not come alive when the heat of the spotlight blazes upon his face; he does not surge into character when the stage is exposed to the audience.

I look out at the spot where I thought I saw Marigold, and now the tears finally spill from my eyes. I can't hold them back anymore. They have been struggling to escape for far too long now. It will appear to the audience that I'm crying for our father, which is exactly what he would have wanted from me, but alas, I've never been that good an actor.

At centre stage, our father is radiant like a gilt-haloed angel, illuminated by multiple spotlights. His casket has been propped upright so that his admirers can bask in the reflected glow of John Lionel Trouper in his final, resplendent glory.

There is a collective gasp from the audience as Wagner's "Flight of the Valkyries" thunders from the loudspeakers that surround the auditorium. It's a bit much if you ask me, but no one did; every detail of John Lionel Trouper's final show has been painstakingly scripted by our father himself.

No one in the audience is going to remember the soundtrack anyway. What they are going to remember — and talk and tweet and blog about, and relay breathlessly to gossip columnists and tabloid vultures — is what happens next.

If there were an Academy Award for Best Actress at a Show Business Funeral, Joan would definitely be nominated for the performance she is delivering right now.

SCENE: JOAN TROUPER has fallen to her knees beside JOHN LIONEL TROUPER's casket, gasping and sobbing and wailing, alternately burying her face in her hands and then raising them toward the heaven of the overhead lights. JOAN's big eyes gush tears as if there is a firehose plugged into the back of her head.

Seriously, how can one woman's tear ducts produce so much water? It's a physiological abnormality that has served Joan well over the years, both onstage and off.

JOAN is channelling all of her heroines in this single climactic scene. There are tones of Bette Davis in Dark Victory …

JOAN TROUPER. Father! Father! Oh, dear, sweet Father!

… and a perfect homage to Joan Crawford's most weepy, impassioned speech in Mildred Pierce.

JOAN TROUPER. Forgive me, Daddy. I'm sorry! I'm so, so sorry!

Positioned to JOAN's left, VIOLET TROUPER stands as if she is astride an imaginary warhorse, like a post-apocalyptic cowgirl. Her punk rock boots are planted firmly on the floorboards, her arms are crossed defiantly, and her biceps and triceps twitch beneath her blue-green tattoos.

And if there were an Academy Award for Best Supporting Actress at a Show Business Funeral, Violet would certainly be in the running as her eyes narrow to serpentine slits and she rasps like Clint Eastwood's Man with No Name, "Bravo, Joan. Bravo." A few whispering voices in the audience echo the word, "Bravo," and they shake their heads at Joan in sync with Violet as a slight smirk cracks through her hardened expression.

Violet's fans are easy to pick out from the rest of the crowd. They are the ones in black leather and torn denim, tall boots and fishnet hose. They are the ones with the tattoos and nose rings and blood-red lipstick and thick circles of black drawn around their eyes, the ones wearing the Kitty Galore T-shirts. Earlier, while waiting for the curtain to open, I could hear a few of them singing the band's newest song, "Push My Button," a catchy three-chord anthem celebrating the power and majesty of the clitoris.

Joan's supporters also tend to stand out from the rank and file; perhaps the easiest way to describe her demographic is to quote the slogan from her short-lived JOAN T™ line of fragrances and cosmetics: "For Drama Queens and Sassy Things of all Colours, Shapes, and Sizes." Some of the fans of her cabaret-club Joan Crawford impersonation have made the trip all the way from Los Angeles just to see Joan perform a different character upon a different stage.

JOAN now delivers her coup de grâce *with a skyward plea, her rhythm and cadence a nearly perfect echo of Vivien Leigh's "With God as my witness …" speech from* Gone with the Wind.

JOAN TROUPER. Why, oh, why? Why us? Why him? Why now?

VIOLET TROUPER. *(muttering)* Gawd! What a drama queen!

JOAN TROUPER. *(wailing)* You shut up, you heartless *bitch*.

I glance over at Olivia, who is holding her face in her hands, not to any dramatic end, but to conceal her embarrassment at her sisters' onstage bickering. There are no fans out there for Olivia; producers like her get the lion's share of the money, but it's the performers like her sisters who get the attention. There are no fans out there for me, either; struggling writers rarely have a cheering section.

On cue, there is another cloudburst from JOAN's dark eyes, webbing her cheeks with mascara-accentuated tributaries.

JOAN TROUPER. Oh, Daddy! Oh, Daddy!

Wailing, JOAN rushes with arms outstretched toward the glowing, beatific-looking body of JOHN LIONEL TROUPER.

There is another gasp from the audience.

Violet shakes her head and rolls her eyes as she grunts, "Good gawd, Joan," then she grabs her sister's shoulders to restrain her, but Joan twists and bucks like an escape artist to break free from Violet's straitjacket grip.

Joan stumbles forward, her arms flailing, frantically grabbing for something, anything, to break her impending fall.

The casket teeters back and forth at the edge of the stage.

There is another gasp from the crowd, so deep and unanimous that it momentarily sucks the oxygen from the theatre. For a moment, I feel as if I might black out.

From stage right, Olivia and I watch in helpless horror. It is like watching an explosion in slow motion, and there is nothing we can do to contain it.

From stage left, Violet springs into action, grabbing the teetering coffin from behind just as it is about to tumble forward. Our father's stiff body falls free from its red satin surroundings and topples over the edge of the stage.

The next collective gasp creates an absolute vacuum. It feels as if all of the oxygen has been sucked from the room.

Olivia wobbles and crumples onto the floorboards. She falls onto her back, her arms and legs splayed wide.

A guy in a rumpled army surplus jacket and khaki pants sidles up to the edge of the stage and begins filming up Olivia's skirt with a small digital video camera. I lunge for him, grab for his camera, but the guy has already spun around and sprinted halfway to the exit doors.

(Here is a reliable prediction: by this evening, Olivia will be featured in a YouTube video titled something like "Trouper Sister Funeral Upskirt!" that will inevitably go viral.)

I've landed sideways, facing stage left, and a feeling of déjà vu overwhelms me. I can see Joan and Violet tangled together, rolling back and forth across the stage floor in a clawing, slapping, no-holds-barred wrestling match. Several people are filming this, too.

(I can see it now: "Trouper Sister Funeral Catfight!" It's going to be a big night for the Troupers on the internet.)

Then I glance over the precipice and see that our father's body is not lying on the auditorium floor where he should have landed; instead, he is somehow hovering above the crowd, glowing supernaturally.

A dazed Olivia sits up, and she marvels at her levitating father. Violet releases Joan from a headlock, and they both look up, too. All of the would-be paparazzi in the audience aim their cameras at John Lionel, who floats just above their heads, radiating bright, warm light.

The spotlight operators have kept their beams trained upon him, and he drifts upon a slow current of fingers and palms, buoyed by his audience, who have lifted his body above their heads. Everyone wants to touch him — some for the first time, all for the last.

Some leave him with tokens of their affections: his pockets are filled with notes and trinkets, and his face, neck, and hands are polka-dotted with pink and red lipstick marks. Others take souvenirs: his golden cravat is untucked from his collar, the drama masks are plucked from his cuffs, the knight's-head ring slips from his finger, and the coat-of-arms buttons are all snapped off from his double-breasted jacket, one by one.

Hand over hand, his body is eventually delivered back to the stage, and the flustered funeral director secures our father back inside his coffin.

Our father's fall and rise has been recorded, too, on phones and tablets and digital cameras. The Troupers are going to break the internet tonight.

Joan, Violet, Olivia, and I pick ourselves up, dust ourselves off, and resume our positions atop the stage.

And maybe it's just a trick of the light, a strange shadow created by the crossing spotlight beams, but I swear that our father has a smirk on his face that wasn't there before.

Scene 4:
The Conditions
(Or: Pushing Buttons)

AS WE MAKE OUR way through the darkened backstage corridor, that tingling, spiders-on-the-neck feeling overtakes me once again, and I glance over my shoulder at the now-empty stage.

That same slender, hooded figure, clad entirely in black, is watching me from behind a fluttering backstage curtain.

I spin around and yelp, "Hey!", but when I blink, the dark figure disappears, once again just a shadow, certainly just a figment of my imagination.

Olivia taps me on the shoulder, and I turn around again.

"You okay?" she asks, genuinely concerned.

"It's nothing," I tell her. "It was nothing."

"Come on, then," she says. "I've arranged for the limo to take the four of us to Trouper Terrace to meet with the lawyer."

"The lawyer?" I hear myself ask.

"Yes," Olivia says. "The sooner we get this over with, the better."

AND NOW THE FOUR of us who remain — Joan, Violet, Olivia, and I — are gathered around the kitchen table at Trouper Terrace. After what just happened onstage at the Orpheum-Galaxie, none of us are able to look one another in the eyes.

The lawyer drops a tape player in the centre of the table, pops a cassette inside, and presses the play button.

After a moment of tape hiss, John Lionel's famous baritone voice rattles the small speaker like the Ghost of Marley in *A Christmas Carol*. "After living such a long and full life, rich with experience and full of recognitions and accolades of every kind, I recognize that my children are the living extensions of my successes, and I would like to provide them with the opportunity to try to reach the summits to which I climbed in my own charmed lifetime."

He pauses for dramatic effect. The sound of tape hiss fills echoes against the kitchen's black-and-white tiles.

"To this end, aside from the natural talents and gifts that have been passed on to my offspring through me, I now bequeath to my surviving children, to be divided equally between them, the following three Trouper family assets."

He pauses again, accompanied by tape hiss.

"Asset Number One: The balance of funds in the Trouper Family accounts."

This won't likely amount to much, since the money originally inherited by our grandmother from her late husband had already dwindled substantially by the time the Troupers mounted our final show together, and whatever was left of that must be nearly gone now, since our father sustained himself from those accounts during the two decades that have passed since then (and, presumably, he also depleted the even greater reserve that our mother inherited from the Royales).

"Asset Number Two: Our family home, Trouper Terrace."

This isn't much of an asset, either. It is obvious that, since our grandmother's death, our father has done nothing to maintain the needy old manor. The mansion's Italianate tower is now leaning at an angle resembling its taller cousin in Pisa, the tiles are falling from the sagging mansard roof, and a family of raccoons has taken up residence beneath the warped and broken floorboards of the wraparound veranda. As we marched with the lawyer through our former home to the kitchen in the back, my sisters and I marvelled at the formerly gleaming hardwood floors and ornate furnishings now coated in a haze of dust, the windows draped with hanging cobwebs like interior shots from a haunted house horror film.

"Asset Number Three: The Trouper-Royale Orpheum-Galaxie Theatre."

Our father's voice squeaks as Olivia presses the pause button on the tape player, and she says in her usual businesslike way, "I've already received an offer from a movie theatre chain to purchase the Orpheum-Galaxie and retrofit it into a high-end movie venue, and a hotel company has expressed interest in acquiring Trouper Terrace to convert it into a luxury spa." Olivia glances around at the rest of us. "So ... all those in favour of accepting these offers?"

In a rare act of unity, the Trouper Siblings all raise our hands at once.

I can't say I'm surprised; none of us has any desire to ever live at Trouper Terrace again, nor to ever perform again atop the Orpheum-Galaxie's stage — except for maybe Joan, but although we all could use the money, she's the Trouper sibling who surely needs it the most. Her spending on Hollywood outfits and vodka martinis must certainly outweigh her income as a Joan Crawford cabaret imitator and occasional B-movie actor, not to mention the insane cost of the L.A. loft that she rents with several other cabaret performers and B-list movie actors.

"Before we get too far ahead of ourselves," the lawyer intones, "there are conditions to be met."

As she reaches to restart the tape, we all lower our hands.

Our father's voice intones ominously, "My children shall freely inherit these funds and properties upon satisfying the following three conditions."

Another dramatic pause, accentuated by the sound of tape hiss.

"Condition Number One: My surviving children must join together and contribute their respective talents to producing one final show. Condition Number Two: The initial run of said production must take place at the Trouper-Royale Orpheum-Galaxie Theatre, and performances must begin within three months of the date of my passing."

Violet reaches out and stabs the stop button on the tape player with a stubby fingernail painted black.

"He thinks he's going to keep directing us onstage even after he's dead?" she yelps, echoing my thoughts almost verbatim. "Well, forget it. I quit acting when I left here, and I'm twice as quit now."

Violet sounds just like Harrison Ford in *Blade Runner* as she delivers that paraphrased line. I am impressed.

"I'm retired from acting, too," I affirm.

"Well, so am I," Olivia says, "but maybe we should listen to the rest of the tape before we make any hasty —"

"If I do a show here myself," Joan says hopefully to the lawyer, "do I still get my share of the inheritance?"

"No," the lawyer says. "He specifically states that you all have to be involved. It's an all-or-nothing deal."

We all exchange glances, looking into one another's eyes for the first time since sitting down at the kitchen table.

"Well, let's hear the rest of it, then," Violet says. She leans forward and presses the play button.

"Condition Number Three," our father thunders. "The aforementioned production must also involve the entire cast of the Trouper Family's previous and final show, specifically, *The Women*, which ran during the month of May 1995 at the Trouper-Royale Orpheum-Galaxie Theatre. All cast members who have not predeceased the director of that show — meaning me, John Lionel Trouper — *must* be included in the production."

Joan stabs the stop button with a lacquered-red fingernail.

"Is he out of his freakin' mind? He wants us to work with Prudence Petty … and Amber Anderson … and, jeezus! Penny Petty? What a little bitch she's grown up to be."

"Hey," Violet says, "I'm willing to work with *you*."

Joan jumps to her feet. "I won't do it. Not if we have to include *them*."

Olivia gets up to stop Joan from storming from the room and says evenly, "One more show and we're free, Joan. One. More. Show."

My sisters are astonished when I also rise to my feet. "Let's do it!" I say, and even I am somewhat surprised by the surety in my own voice. "Let's put on this show." I look at Joan, then at Violet, and then at Olivia, and with an intensity that I was never able to summon onstage, I say, "We can do this. Let's prove it to him. And, more importantly, let's prove it to ourselves."

There is another reason that I want to revive the show, but I'm not going to mention it to my sisters. Olivia will tell me that I'm being irrational, Joan will scoff and call me desperate, and Violet will advise me to just let it go and move on … and they would all probably be right. Marigold surely died along with our mother in the crash after our final performance of *The Women*, and reviving the show will certainly not also revive her … but still, her gentle voice whispers in my ear, "You can't go forward until you go back."

I reach out and press the play button, and the voice of our father proclaims grandly, "My beautiful, talented daughters … and son … my brilliant progeny, you must put yourselves back onstage where you all belong. You must put aside the minor slights of the past and restore the great, shining legacy that was … that *is* … the Trouper Family."

The tape hiss that fills the room sounds like applause, but also like the sound of water rushing around the wreckage of a small black car.

The lawyer takes a final jab at the stop button and says curtly, "Please contact me as soon as the conditions of your father's last will and testament have been met, and then we can discuss the disposition of assets and distribution of funds."

She exits, leaving the cassette inside the tape player atop the kitchen table and the four surviving members of the Fabulous Trouper Quintuplets sitting together around it, each of us waiting for one of the others to deliver the opening line, to break the silence that fills the room.

I imagine that my sisters have been struck mute by the same line that has left me speechless: "You must put aside the minor slights of the past."

Only John Lionel Trouper could describe the destruction he left in his wake as "minor."

Only our father could portray the injuries he inflicted upon us as "slights."

Scene 5:

The Immaculate Conception

(Or: Five Fingers Waving for the Camera)

OUR EARLIEST APPEARANCE TOGETHER as the Fabulous Trouper Quintuplets was not on stage but on film or, to be more precise, on videotape. This particular video is a grainy Betamax recording, which was cutting-edge technology in 1977, the year that we were born.

Almost everywhere our father went during this period of his life, he had a video camera filming from an inauspicious location, capturing raw material for the documentary that would one day be made about his exceptional life and stellar career.

INT. TROUPER TERRACE, LIVING ROOM – DAY.

JOHN LIONEL TROUPER, with a fat cigar hanging from the corner of his mouth and a glass of bourbon in one hand, is prancing around his pregnant young wife, LILY ROYALE-TROUPER, who is lounging in a La-Z-Boy recliner.

JOHN LIONEL TROUPER

Five babies! Five! Who's your leading man, baby? Who's your leading man?

John Lionel waves five fingers for the camera and then pounds his chest, Tarzan-style; he is strong, potent, and virile, and he still deserves top billing.

JOHN LIONEL TROUPER

(Channelling George C. Scott as General Patton)

My men broke through the front lines, didn't they? And how! My sperm are like shock troops. Send in the Marines! Five babies. Five!

Lily pats her swollen belly and smiles.

LILY ROYALE-TROUPER

I know, John Lionel, I know. They're right here.

On the videotape, Mom is twenty years old, only two years older than my sisters and I were when she died. It's funny (well, perhaps *peculiar* is a better word) how this younger version of our mother somehow seems more accomplished, more dignified, more elegant, and more mature than my sisters and I will ever be. The grown-up versions of Joan, Violet, Olivia, and I are now just funhouse mirror-distorted versions of the self-conscious, approval-seeking child actors we once were, but on that Betamax tape, our mother radiates the calm, easy feminine charm of Ingrid Bergman and the regal self-confidence and presence of Grace Kelly, seasoned with dashes of Barbara Stanwyck's sass and Ava Gardner's brass.

It was certainly this combination of charms that helped nineteen-year-old Lily Royale win the lead female role of Maggie in the 1976 summer production of *Cat on a Hot Tin Roof* at the Royale Orpheum-Galaxie Theatre — although it probably didn't hurt her chances that her parents owned the theatre. It's too bad that no film exists of our mother's performance; she received consistently excellent reviews from the critics, and even a Best Actress nomination.

The play was directed by forty-four-year-old stage veteran John Lionel Trouper, who cast himself opposite Lily Royale in the starring role as Brick. One critic grumbled, "At his age, John Lionel Trouper probably would have been better cast as Big Daddy," but there was always a glimmer of the child star he had once been in anything our father ever did, so according to most other accounts he was able to play the younger character more than convincingly.

John Lionel had directed his first play, *The Cocktail Party* (also starring himself), at the Orpheum-Galaxie a decade earlier, and the owners of the theatre, Herbert and Frances Royale, were so happy with the box office returns that they invited our father to become the theatre's permanent artistic director. He soon developed the habit of casting the most attractive young woman who auditioned for any show as the romantic interest of the male lead, who was invariably played by himself, and as a result,

John Lionel had a new affair each summer with whomever he had cast as his opposite. As such, no one in the theatre business was particularly surprised when his romantic partner of 1976 turned out to be Lily Royale.

Observers *were* somewhat astonished when, rather than breaking up with her shortly after the final performance of *Cat on a Hot Tin Roof* (as had been his usual summer theatre tradition), John Lionel instead proposed to Lily Royale, and they were married soon thereafter. This initial surprise waned significantly, however, when we Trouper Quintuplets were born on May 25, 1977, well within a nine-month window of John Lionel Trouper and Lily Royale's final performance as Brick and Maggie.

At least our father decided to "do the right thing" when he discovered that our mother was pregnant with his children, or perhaps Herbert and Frances Royale coerced him into doing it. In the marriage announcement in the local newspaper, Lily was described as being "on the cusp of her twenties" to avoid directly mentioning that our mother was only nineteen years old when her affair with our father began. Somehow, to the chattering socialites who clustered around the Royales like fawning courtiers, this subtlety of semantics erased any hint of scandal that might otherwise have emanated from the betrothed couple's twenty-five-year age difference.

In our parents' official engagement photograph, our mother holds a bouquet of roses in front of her abdomen, perhaps to conceal the evidence of my sisters and me already growing inside her. Her parents, Herbert and Frances Royale, stand behind our father with prim, tight-lipped socialite smiles painted on their faces, each with a hand clamped firmly on one of John Lionel's shoulders. Our father's mother, Chrysanthemum Trouper, stands an arm's length away from the bride-to-be, averting her eyes and leaning away from Lily Royale as if repelled by a force opposite to gravity.

In every photograph taken of her during and after her days with the Ziegfeld Follies, Chrysanthemum Trouper is seen grinning like the Cheshire cat, but in our parents' wedding photograph she scowls as if someone switched her bourbon for kerosene. Perhaps she had tried, as she always did, to purchase a better outcome for her son, but the Royales' fortune made Chrysanthemum Trouper's inherited money seem like nickels under the cushions of their great room daybeds, so the marriage of the Frances and Herbert's only daughter to Chrysanthemum's only son would happen with or without her approval.

As a wedding gift, Herbert and Frances Royale handed over the deed to the theatre, with its name officially changed to the *Trouper*-Royale Orpheum-Galaxie, and as a result of this generous gift, our father would go on to direct and act in some of the greatest plays of his career on the stage of the venerable theatre. He would also continue dallying with the majority of his female counterparts backstage — and sometimes onstage, or in the seats of the auditorium, or up against the polished brass balcony railing — all under the wizened gaze of the silent cherubs and gargoyles perched around the perimeter of the auditorium.

On the Betamax tape, though, John Lionel plays the proud, over-the-moon, newlywed father-to-be to maximum effect, almost as if he's in a Keystone Cops comedy. Our mother, in contrast, portrays the devoted, loving, newlywed mother-to-be with poised dignity. It's a shame that she quit acting when we were born because, with those rare, camera-ready qualities, Lily Royale-Trouper could have had a career that outshone her husband's.

JOHN LIONEL TROUPER
(To the camera, rather than
to Lily herself)
Five babies, Lily. And they'll
all be stars, all five of them! The
Fabulous Trouper Sisters! They'll
be like the Dionne Quintuplets,
but even more famous.

Lily rubs her belly.

LILY ROYALE-TROUPER
Well, maybe without the part where
the government takes them away
and makes them into a tourist
attraction, huh?

John Lionel feigns a pout.

JOHN LIONEL TROUPER
I'm just excited, that's all.

LILY ROYALE-TROUPER
I know, John Lionel. And I'm glad.

It still seems funny to me (well, no, *peculiar* again) that all five of us — Joan, Violet, Olivia, Marigold, and I — are in this scene together with our parents. We are inside our mother, not much larger than the five fingers our father waves for the camera. That grainy, distorted Betamax recording was, technically speaking, our first live appearance together as the Fabulous Trouper Quintuplets.

It was our second filmed appearance, though, that would seal our five fates: the live television broadcast of our birth.

Scene 6:

The Live Broadcast Event of the Year

(Or: You Can't Say "Penis" on Public Television)

IF YOU WATCH IT on YouTube, it looks a lot like the birth scenes you see on TV shows all the time now, with the sweat-glistening mother huffing and grunting and occasionally stifling screams, the done-this-a-hundred-times-before doctor saying, "Push … push now … deep breaths … deep breaths …," and the fretting, mostly useless father offering encouragements like, "You're doing great, baby. You're doing great."

The cameras were set up so we couldn't be seen emerging from our mother; it was television in the late seventies, and although many barriers had been broken by shows like *All in the Family* and *Saturday Night Live*, they couldn't (and wouldn't) actually show a baby emerging from a woman's vagina, let alone *five* babies. So, you don't see much of our mother at all; it's mostly our father mugging and narrating for the camera. John Lionel Trouper is the star of the show, as usual.

Despite her performance being almost entirely off camera,

though, our mother was quite a trouper herself, ensuring that the delivery of all five of her children didn't take even one minute longer than the hour time slot we had been allotted.

They filmed us using a then state-of-the-art RCA TK45 television camera, so at least the video quality is slightly better than the Betamax.

INT. NIAGARA GENERAL HOSPITAL, MATERNITY WARD – NIGHT.

JOHN LIONEL TROUPER

(grandly)

The first of the Fabulous Trouper Sisters to join our family's entertainment legacy is … Joan!

JOHN LIONEL holds up the glistening, swaddled baby for the camera – and the TV audience – to adore.

JOAN has a full head of thick, dark hair, and she isn't crying; she makes more of a cooing sound, like a baby dove. Although her dark eyes cannot yet see, she seems to look right into the TV camera lens and into everyone's souls on the other side. Only minutes into her life, Joan already seems destined for stardom.

John Lionel hands Joan to the ATTRACTIVE NURSE, who holds up the baby for the camera, like a spokesmodel on a daytime television game show displaying a jug of fabric softener.

John Lionel nudges the Attractive Nurse away from the camera.

JOHN LIONEL TROUPER

And here comes our second Fabulous Trouper Sister! You're doing great, Lily. You're doing great …

VIOLET enters the world screeching and thrashing like a netted wildcat. Her few wet, wispy strands of blond hair stand on end; John Lionel tries to brush them down with the palm of his hand, to make his second-born pretty for the camera, but her hairs spring right back up again.

JOHN LIONEL TROUPER

(To the Doctor)

Huh … so I guess they're not identical quints then, eh? Like the Dionne Quintuplets?

DOCTOR

(Painfully aware of the camera)

No, your babies are fraternal quintuplets. Each egg was fertilized by a different sperm.

JOHN LIONEL TROUPER

That means that my sperm are really potent, right? Super sperm! (his tone turns sober) Still, I was really hoping for –

DOCTOR

Fraternal quintuplets are extremely rare. So, you ought to get some attention for that, I imagine.

(back to Lily)

Okay, Lily, one more time.

LILY ROYALE-TROUPER (O.C.)

Ooooooh! Oooooooooh!

Distracted by the guttural sounds of his third offspring already emerging, John Lionel forgets to introduce Violet to the camera. He absently hands the shrieking, tomato-red baby to the Attractive Nurse, who takes a moment to smile for the camera before setting down the screaming Violet.

ATTRACTIVE NURSE

Gosh, this one's got a good pair of lungs, doesn't she?

The video of our births gets a lot of hits on YouTube, mostly because of the Attractive Nurse, who, shortly afterward, began starring in TV commercials for diapers, baby food, and disinfecting products, which eventually led to her being cast as Nurse Monica Holloway on *Hollywood Hospital*. She has played the role for thirty-eight years now, making her the eighteenth-longest-serving actor on an American daytime drama, between Eric Braden as Victor Newman on *The Young and The Restless* and Patricia Bruder as Ellen Lowell on *As the World Turns*.

The Trouper Quintuplets are happy to have helped launch her long and illustrious acting career, especially my sister Olivia, who recently scored major points with the CEO at AMUSEMENT ELEVEN™ by convincing the now-grandmotherly version of the Attractive Nurse to make a campy guest appearance on one of their sitcoms that had been struggling in the ratings, which opened the floodgates for a rush of other campy guest appearances, which ultimately saved the show.

And speaking of Olivia ...

After more sounds of childbirth in progress, John Lionel holds up Olivia for the TV camera.

JOHN LIONEL TROUPER

Ladies and gentlemen, presenting the third member of the Fabulous Trouper Sisters ... OLIVIA!

Unlike her sisters, Olivia simply cries like a normal newborn baby. John Lionel hands her to the Attractive Nurse.

LILY ROYALE-TROUPER (O.C.)

Ooooooooh! Oh God oh God oh God ...

```
John Lionel looks antsy and distressed because
it is taking a longer time for the fourth
Fabulous Trouper Sister to join her siblings
in the outside world, and empty time seems
disproportionately long when there is a camera
rolling or an audience watching. Desperately,
John Lionel decides to make a speech.

                    JOHN LIONEL TROUPER
            Our five daughters will be a
            great troupe of actresses. They
            are inheriting a great legacy;
            they will represent the fourth
            generation of a grand family of
            entertainers.
```

Although our father's tendency to exaggerate is legendary, both onstage and off, especially in service of a good story, this statement is accurate; our legacy as entertainers really does go back four generations. As a small child, our grandmother performed alongside her parents in the music halls of London, England, in a musical comedy routine; as children, Joan, Violet, Olivia, Marigold, and I would gather around her lounging chair, and she would retell the story in her gravelly, bourbon-and-cigar-seasoned voice.

"As I may have told you before, my loves, many of the songs and jokes in our act revolved around my mother and father's poor parenting skills, and we had one song-and-dance number called, 'If You Don't Like it Here, You Can Get Right Out.' There was a bit where my father would throw a suitcase at me, and it was supposed to hit my shoulder and knock me over sideways, and I was supposed to exaggerate the force of the blow by cart-wheeling across the stage. Anyway, that night my father had knocked back a few more snorts of gin than usual, and he threw the bag early, before I was in position, and I got hit square in the face. I fell backward and couldn't tumble into my fall like I usually did, so my head bounced off the boards, and the suitcase landed right on my face."

Like any good live performer, Chrysanthemum Trouper would pause at this climactic moment to wait for her audience's reaction.

"Well," our grandmother would then continue, "the rubes just about died laughing that night. They thought that this was just part of the show, that the blood was just HP sauce or something, and that my father carrying me offstage was the 'you can get right out' part of the number. Mother and Father kept dancing and singing the song right up to the end. They brought me around with some smelling salts, wiped the blood off my face, and I went back out and finished the show. That's what you do, right, my loves? The show must go on. The show must always go on."

At this point, she would pause for a sip of brandy or a pull from her Cuban cigar.

"Anyway, by the time the suitcase-in-the-face incident happened, I had collected a lot of cuts and bruises, both onstage and off, and I was growing tired of it all. So, I nicked some money from the cash box, and I snuck out through the dressing room window and down the fire escape. I slept that night in an alley under some newspapers, like I was Charlie Chaplin's Tramp character, and the next morning I bought a steerage ticket on a boat to New York City."

On cue, one of us would invariably ask, "And that's how we all became the Troupers?"

"That's right, my loves. When I arrived at Ellis Island in New

York and they asked me my name, I didn't want to use my real name because I didn't want anyone tracing me back to my parents in England. But I did want to keep performing — it's in my blood, I suppose — so I told them it was Chrysanthemum Trouper. I made it up on the spot — I thought that it sounded like a good name for an aspiring actress."

Which would beg another inevitable question: "And that's when you joined the Ziegfeld Follies, Grandmother?"

"Yes, my dears. A lot of Ziegfeld Girls went on to fame and fortune when they were discovered performing in the Follies — Virginia Biddle, Marion Davies, Paulette Goddard, Barbara Stanwyck, Louise Brooks — so I thought I would give it a go, too. I danced from 1929 until 1931, until the Depression hit hard and the show fell apart. But I got lucky then, too — out of all of the other girls up there smiling and dancing, your grandfather chose me. He proposed to me right after the show one night, right there in the dressing room in front of all of the other girls."

"And you said yes!"

"Of course I did, my loves. What girl would have turned down a proposal from Herschel Pennyblood?"

I suppose it's a good thing that our grandmother said yes; otherwise, we Trouper Quintuplets might not exist at all.

In the delivery room, MARIGOLD has still not emerged; John Lionel Trouper glances anxiously at the clock on the wall and continues his impromptu speech.

JOHN LIONEL TROUPER

And we will raise this fourth generation of performers to be great! Our daughters' inherited talents — their genetic destinies — will be supplemented and nourished with nothing but the best. Our children will see no film made after the 1950s. They will be raised on the classics, the films of the Golden Age, when actors could actually act. They will be exposed to nothing but the finest, truest performances!

He said it, and he did it. Unlike many of our father's other grand proclamations, this one he actually followed through on. In order to help us to fulfill our "genetic destinies," strict rules were created and enforced:

— The Trouper Quintuplets were not allowed to watch any film made after the 1950s.
— We were taken only to plays pre-approved by our father.
— We were not allowed to watch contemporary television shows, only episodes on tape, pre-selected by our father from the "Golden Age of Television."
— To keep our development pure, we would not attend public school; we would instead be homeschooled around our rehearsal and performance schedule (a task that would be assigned to our mother, of course).

The next wave of John Lionel's impassioned speech is interrupted when Lily cries out.

LILY ROYALE-TROUPER (O.C.)

Oh God. Oh God. Ohhhhhhh God!

Soon John Lionel is holding Marigold, who wears an amazed expression, as if she already finds the world both wonderful and terrifying at the same time, as if she already sees what is coming.

MARIGOLD TROUPER

Oooooooooh.

The Attractive Nurse takes her, and Marigold seems to smile.

And now, ladies and gentlemen, here is the moment no one has been waiting for: my own inauspicious debut.

JOHN LIONEL TROUPER

(To the camera)

And now, prepare to meet the Fifth Fabulous Trouper Sister … Miss Bette Trouper!

LILY ROYALE-TROUPER (O.C.)

OOOOOOOOOOOOOOOOOOOOOOOOOOOOOH!

JOHN LIONEL TROUPER

Holy shit! Sweet mother of … does she have a fucking PENIS?

DIRECTOR (O.C.)

(Hollering to the TV crew)

Whoa, Nelly! Cut! Cut! Pull the plug! Shut it down!

(hollering at John Lionel)

What's wrong with you, man? You can't say "fucking penis" on public television!

And with that, our John Lionel Trouper went down in the annals of entertainment history as the first person to ever utter the phrase "fucking penis" in any public broadcast medium. Despite this dubious claim to fame, however, the live television debut of the Fabulous Trouper Quintuplets didn't get the high ratings that our father was hoping for.

It may have been that our potential audience was distracted that day, since we were born on May 25, 1977, the same day that *Star Wars* was released. It may have been that our live birth was broadcast at 3:00 a.m. on public television, and there wouldn't have been much of an audience anyway. Nevertheless, I've always felt like our father blamed me personally for delaying the rise to stardom that he had planned for his offspring.

Even in the opening moments of my life, I was a resounding disappointment to the Great John Lionel Trouper. His dream of directing the Fabulous Trouper Sisters to stardom was destroyed by one waggle of my infant penis, and I believe that he held this against me for the rest of his life, even though it was his chromosome that decided my sex.

At least they decided to change my name from Bette to Errol, which was a nice conciliatory gesture.

And I'm sure Bette Davis was relieved.

Scene 7:

The Scallywags

(Or: A Loving Tribute)

JOHN LIONEL WAS NOT merely grandstanding for the television camera when he declared that his offspring would be raised to fulfill our genetic destinies as the fourth generation of an entertainment dynasty and that we would see no film or television show made after the 1950s. While other children of the late seventies and early eighties were watching Big Bird, Oscar the Grouch, and Bert and Ernie on their families' RCA and Electrohome and Zenith colour TV sets, we Trouper Quintuplets were raised solely on episodes of our father's first show, *The Scallywags* (and sometimes its "inspiration," *Our Gang*), projected directly from the original film reels onto a pull-down movie screen in the basement of Trouper Terrace.

Since we rarely left the confines of the estate, and because we played only with one another, we never really knew what we were missing. Our improvised dramas and comedies were played out upon the veranda of Trouper Terrace or the rehearsal stage our father had built in the basement, and by the tender age of five years old, each of us had already been unconsciously typecast: Joan was the Beautiful Queen, Violet was the Rough-and-Tumble Tomboy, Marigold was the Kind-Hearted Fairy, Olivia was the Bespectacled Brain. And me? I was the loyal horse. Or the loyal dog. Or the loyal servant boy. Or whatever else my sisters — and especially our father — required me to be.

After absorbing a constant barrage of *Scallywags* and *Our Gang* films, we soon began recreating the plot lines ourselves when we played together atop our stages. And perhaps this was our father's intention all along.

IN 1938, WHEN OUR father was five years old, the *Our Gang* (aka *The Little Rascals*) short films were at the height of their popularity. The kindergarten-aged John Lionel loved the slapstick antics of the children in the *Our Gang* films, and despite indirectly possessing his industrialist father's enormous wealth, he nevertheless related to the Little Rascals' underclass but egalitarian gang of black and white boys and girls, and he rooted quite seriously for them in their comedic battles against rich kids, bullies, and mean ol' grown-ups.

I'll give our father this: his love for *Our Gang* as a child may have had a profound effect on the development of his adult personality; he never cared about the colour of a person's skin, the amount of money in their wallet, who their parents were, where they came from, their political persuasion, their sexual orientation, or any of the other categories that often cause one human being to be biased toward or against another human being. As far as John Lionel was concerned, if you were fun, interesting, talented, attractive — and, most importantly, flattering and subservient to John Lionel — you were in, and if you were none of these things, you were out. It was as simple as that.

By the time he was five years old, John Lionel had already been doted upon enough to know that he had charm and charisma to burn. So, he began to wheedle his mother (and his father, on the rare occasions that Herschel Pennyblood was actually home with his family) to take him to Hal Roach Studios in Hollywood to join the cast of *Our Gang*. His cajoling gradually escalated from smiling sweetly, batting his eyelashes, and saying "Pleeeeease?" in a sing-song voice to whining, pouting, and moping, and finally to shrieking, wailing, foot-stomping tantrums. When Chrysanthemum Trouper could take no more, she in turn pressured her husband in a similarly escalating fashion, and through his financial connections in the movie business, Herschel Pennyblood called in some favours to procure an audition for their only son.

One of Pennyblood's secretaries made the arrangements and booked the train tickets, and Chrysanthemum and John Lionel arrived at Hal Roach Studios in Hollywood on June 1, 1938, which, as it turned out, was one day after Roach signed a deal with MGM that sold them the rights to the *Our Gang* unit, including the contracts for the actors and writers, for $25,000. If this hadn't happened, would our father have joined Spanky, Alfalfa, Darla, Buckwheat, and Porky as the sixth member of the most popular all-child cast of all time? Cinematic history will never know.

From the narrative that Marigold and I were able to cobble together, based on listening in secretly on adult conversations and covertly digging through documents in our father's office, what happened next went something like this:

As our young, beautiful grandmother and our cute-as-a-button five-year-old father sat on the curb outside Hal Roach Studios, waiting for a cab to take them back to their hotel room, a tall, thin young man in overalls ambled out through the gates and sat down beside them.

"Why so sad, little fellah?" he said, reaching over and mussing little John Lionel's wavy hair. Then he turned to Chrysanthemum. "Why so glum, miss? It can't be that bad, can it?"

Tears trickled from the former showgirl's expressive eyes. "I brought my son here all the way from New York so he could audition for a role in *Our Gang*, only to discover that the whole production's been sold to MGM."

"Yeah, I know all about that," said the lean young man. "I was a cameraman for *Our Gang*, and I just found out today that I'm not getting shipped over there with everyone else. They've already got their own crew at MGM, so as of today, I am officially unemployed."

"Oh," whispered Chrysanthemum, "I'm sorry."

"Naw, it's fine!" the cameraman said. "I've already got another job lined up. I know a guy who is going to film some one-reelers up in Niagara Falls, on the Canadian side of the river. He can dodge some taxes that way, and they're not as strict about permits and such up there."

"Canada, you say? Will it be a movie about Eskimos? Or Mounties? Or ... let me guess ... the Gold Rush!"

"Naw, we're making another batch of kids' movies ... kinda like *Our Gang*, actually."

"Like a sequel?"

"Well, more like a *copy*, if you wanna be honest about it. Or, if you wanna be completely honest, this series will be a counterfeit, a fake, a rip-off. But work is work, right? A man's gotta eat. And they've got distribution deals already, so they're gonna make some money."

"Gosh," said Chrysanthemum, blinking more tears from her dark, glistening eyes. "I don't suppose that you could ..." She looked away from the young cameraman. "No, no, I ... I don't want to impose."

Taking the cue from his former-showgirl mother, John Lionel also squeezed some tears from his own dark, glistening eyes.

"Lemme guess," the cameraman said, "you're wondering if I might be willing to put in a good word for your tyke here. Am I right?"

"Well," said our young grandmother, sniffling, wiping away tears, and then smiling at the cameraman, "if you're sure it isn't too much of an imposition. Of course, I ... we ... would be very grateful."

The cameraman pulled a card from the pocket in the bib of his overalls and handed it to Chrysanthemum Trouper. "Shooting doesn't begin until early August, so there's plenty of time for everyone to get to know each other."

"Oh, thank you! Thank you so much! You are a very kind man. A true gentleman, to be sure."

"My pleasure, miss, I'm sure." He winked. "Say, where are you staying? Maybe we could share a ride."

AND SO IT CAME to pass that, upon their joyful reunion in New York City, Herschel Pennyblood departed this mortal world, his soul freed from his body while gently making love to his beautiful, young former-showgirl wife ... if you have faith in the "official" version of events, that is. If, however, you believe the tea-and-biscuit busybodies and the muckraking tabloid vultures of the time, the story is that he suffered a massive heart attack while our grandmother rode him like a wild cowgirl atop a crazed bucking bronco.

Some of the more imaginative accounts claim that the wealthy, elderly industrialist was found naked, his ankles and wrists secured with binder twine to a Queen Anne–style dining room chair, his body stiff with rigor mortis, his helmeted private still standing erect. The official reports of the attending ambulance personnel and police officers make note of none of these sordid details, but our grandmother has vehemently denied that any hush money ever changed hands.

In the beginning of July 1938, the newly widowed Chrysanthemum Trouper packed up her belongings, her young son, and her huge bundle of inherited money and moved to their new estate overlooking the Niagara River, and by the end of the month they were settled into Trouper Terrace as if they had always lived there.

In August, production began on the first of many one-reel short films in *The Scallywags* series, featuring young John Lionel as Sparky, the cheeky-yet-cherubic leader whose sidekicks included Elf Elfy, Marla, Barleycorn, and Piggy.

The Scallywags was indeed a blatant rip-off of (or, as our father would put it in later interviews, a "loving tribute to") *Our Gang*, yet the short film series nevertheless became unexpectedly popular, despite the fact that the filmmakers were copying the best of the *Our Gang* films almost shot for shot. If the Little Rascals had a kids' version of a horse racetrack, racing rickety handmade carts pulled by their pet dogs, in the 1923 film *Derby Day*, then the Scallywags would do the same thing again on the streets of Niagara Falls in 1938. If Spanky, Alfalfa, Darla, Buckwheat, and Porky brought the house down in a theatre review in 1935's *Beginner's Luck*, then Sparky, Elf Elfy, Marla, Barleycorn, and Piggy would do the same in 1940. And did Sparky go over the Falls inside a barrel? Of course he did!

Although *The Scallywags* films were rarely shown in the United States (to avoid copyright infringement charges), Sparky and his gang of pint-sized miscreants were especially loved in Canada, where the series was filmed, but also in France, Belgium, and Holland, as the minimal dialogue was overdubbed by recent French- and Dutch-speaking immigrants who were fleeing depression and war in Europe and were thus willing to provide their translation services to the filmmakers for very "reasonable" compensation. As such, young John Lionel had indeed become an "international movie star," and *The Scallywags* was a bona fide hit.

Until it wasn't anymore.

By the time the series ended in 1945, *The Scallywags* was well past its best before date. The movie-loving public found the winking, wisecracking, chubby-cheeked five-year-old version of Sparky to be cute and funny, and the nine-year-old version's antics were still mostly amusing, but they saw the thirteen-year-old Sparky as smug, maudlin, and bloated. The actor playing Barleycorn was on the verge of sixteen; he had grown to a height of almost six feet, and his mustache stubble was visible on camera beneath his makeup. "Cute little Marla" had developed hips and breasts that could no longer be concealed beneath her baby doll dresses, and Elf Elfy's long-standing crush on Marla, which had been adorable during the early years, now seemed creepy and vaguely predatory when played out by a postpubescent teenaged boy.

In the *Our Gang* series, when the child actors grew too old for their roles, they were inevitably replaced by younger children. Why did the producers of *The Scallywags* fail to imitate the original in this one way? Because John Lionel enjoyed being an "international movie star," and Chrysanthemum could afford to keep her son happy by funding the production well after it ceased to be profitable.

The Scallywags finally ground to an overdue halt when the last movie theatre on the distribution list refused to screen the series any longer. And that probably should have been the end of it ... but for me and my sisters, it was only the beginning.

Scene 8:

The NEW Scallywags

(Or: Typecasting)

WHEN THE PRODUCERS FINALLY abandoned *The Scallywags*, Chrysanthemum and John Lionel purchased the scripts for practically nothing. This turned out to be a wise investment (for a little while, anyway) because, in 1982, Hanna-Barbera produced a Saturday morning cartoon version of *The Little Rascals* on network television, which in turn caused many coattail-riding, low-budget local TV stations to re-air the original *Our Gang* films, which in turn caused our father to decide that the time was right for a stage revival of *The Scallywags*, featuring his own offspring.

In *The NEW Scallywags* plays, Sparky (who was "based on" *The Little Rascals*' Spanky) was played by Joan, who our father figured had the most natural aptitude for the role. So, Sparky was renamed Sparkle, and Joan was cast as the female version of the role made famous by John Lionel Trouper himself. It was also at this moment that Joan was officially anointed as our father's Favourite Child, a role that she plays to this day.

As the "girliest" of his girls, Marigold was cast in the lone original female role of Marla (*The Scallywags*' clone of *The Little Rascals*' Darla). Our father allowed Marigold to wear her gold angel wings in her scenes, which delighted both Marigold and our mostly elderly audiences.

John Lionel's scrappiest daughter, Violet, was a shoo-in for the part of Miss Barleycorn (the knockoff version of the lanky Buckwheat). The nostalgic crowd loved Violet's messy, spiky hair and her messy, spiky tomboy persona.

Olivia got the part of Piggy (whose name was changed to Puppy after a rare moment of protest from Olivia), and audiences found her habit of constantly pushing her glasses up her nose to be almost as adorable as Joan's lisp, Marigold's wings, and Violet's dirt-stained elbows and knees.

I was cast as Elf Elfy (*The Scallywags*' version of Alfalfa), and my role was reduced with each production because audiences found my sisters' larger-than-life characters more appealing than my own introverted onstage demeanour, and our father, as director, let me know it. In the final episodes of *The NEW Scallywags*, my character mostly just stood in the background holding things while my sisters competed with one another to draw the biggest laughs.

Our father was a great director in that respect: he cast us in the roles that we had naturally assumed for ourselves when we acted out our own versions of *Scallywags* and *Little Rascals* stories upon our stages at Trouper Terrace, and as a result the reviewers loved us, too. The much-loved theatre critic of an international news magazine raved:

> *The NEW Scallywags* is a fun, nostalgic romp down memory lane! Despite their tender age, the Trouper

> Quintuplets are already gifted character actors, with impeccable comedic timing and nuanced delivery. Five stars for *The NEW Scallywags!*

However, the praise was not unanimous. Another well-known critic, known more for her vitriol than her praise, grumbled:

> *The NEW Scallywags* is nothing more than John Lionel Trouper enslaving his own children to resurrect a product that was tired and derivative (and, dare I say, a blatant copyright infringement) the first time through. Do me — and yourself! — a favour and skip this dull and dated retread.

Thankfully, the positive reviews outnumbered the negative, and soon enough, legions of nostalgic grandparents were making pilgrimages to the Orpheum-Galaxie with their children and grandchildren in tow to relive something that vaguely resembled the happy memories of their youths. *The NEW Scallywags* ran for over half a year, playing to mostly-full houses, and our father was overjoyed with the box office receipts.

It was May 25, 1983, the day of our collective sixth birthday, when it all ended. Joan, Violet, Marigold, Olivia, and I were in our costumes as Sparkle, Miss Barleycorn, Marla, Puppy, and Elf Elfy, and atop a backstage catering table, in addition to the usual trays of deli meats and sliced cheese and dinner rolls for making sandwiches, there was a huge birthday cake with six large candles on top, which had just been carried in by our smiling mother.

My sisters and I had gathered around the cake, wide-eyed, the light from the candles flickering on our faces, when our father wandered into the scene, gripping in one hand the cease-and-desist order from Hanna-Barbera and King World Productions.

"Well," our father sighed, "we had a good run, kids, but this letter says that *The NEW Scallywags* has to end now."

Joan, Violet, and Olivia's voices joined together in a chorus of, "Why, Daddy?"

There was an edge in our mother's voice as she muttered, "Go ahead. Explain it to them."

Our father didn't miss a beat. "Well, it's complicated, kids, but it's okay. We had a good run, and this is just the beginning of great things for you children, you'll see. Now, blow out your birthday candles."

Together, the five of us easily extinguished the six candles. Our mother began cutting the cake.

Olivia worried, "Don't we have to wait until after the show to eat it?"

Marigold fretted, "What if we get icing on our costumes?"

A thousand-watt smile broke across our father's face. "You know what? It's your birthday. We aren't going to perform today. Enjoy your birthday cake, and then just go play. Go have some fun. You kids deserve it."

Joan was still concerned. "But what about all the people who bought tickets?"

"We'll give them refunds," our father assured us. "Now go play. It's your birthday."

Joan and Violet scampered out onto the stage, likely to play a queen and some sort of superhero, respectively. Olivia followed along to act as the director/mediator when the two biggest personalities of the five of us eventually clashed.

Marigold and I hid ourselves away in the folds of the black backstage curtains, and, as we had become very adept at doing, we remained absolutely still and silent as we listened in on our parents' subsequent conversation.

Our mother glared icily at our father. "So, does this mean that you're going to just let them be children again, John Lionel?"

"But they aren't just children," our father thundered. "They are much more than that. They are *my* children. They are —"

"*Our* children."

"They are performers. They are actors. They are the Fabulous Trouper Quintuplets. They are —"

"Extensions of your own ego," our mother hissed.

"Really, Lily? You want to have this fight again?"

Then John Lionel glanced over to stage left, to where our mother had set up a video camera to record us blowing out our birthday candles, and his demeanour and tone instantly changed.

"Oh, Lily, my love," he oozed, "I know that you're just being protective. You're a wonderful mother, and you know I appreciate everything that you do for our children."

He strode casually away from the running camera and toward the catering table, saying, "But you also know that I only want what's best for them, too."

Then, facing both our mother and the camera, he picked up two forks from the catering table and stabbed the tines of each fork into a dinner roll. "But our children are not ordinary," he continued. "They're special. Don't you agree?"

Our mother sighed. "Well, of course I agree ... it's just that —"

With the dinner rolls attached to the forks like feet and the handle of a fork in each hand, our father caused the dinner rolls to kick and dance across the catering table, imitating Charlie

Chaplin's famous routine in *The Gold Rush*.

In spite of herself, a smile cracked through our mother's angry expression. "One of these days, John Lionel," she said, "that charm of yours is going to run out. And then what are we going to do?"

Scene 9:

The Show Must Go On

(Or: A Hard Act to Follow)

WITH THE ABRUPT CANCELLATION of *The NEW Scallywags*, our father had to act quickly to refill the seats in the unexpectedly empty auditorium of the Orpheum-Galaxie, so he announced a revival of one of his most successful adult plays, *The Cocktail Party* by T.S. Eliot.

Initially, our mother was delighted. "Oh, John Lionel," she cheered, "that's a wonderful idea! I would love to play Celia Coplestone this time around!"

"Oh, that's a nice idea in theory, Lily, but not this time," our father grumbled. "I'm going to recruit the cast of my previous production to reprise their roles."

"I would love to get back onstage again," said our mother hopefully.

"It's been seven years, Lily," our father said coolly. "This show needs to get up and running fast, and I'm not sure that you're ready for that."

"But, John Lionel, I —"

"I won Best Actor and Best Director for that show, Lily," our father interrupted. "And, as the saying goes, 'You don't mess with success.'"

Our mother deflated like a leaking balloon. "I suppose you're going to cast Pretty Slutty as Celia, then?"

"'Little pitchers have big ears, Lily," our father said sternly, glancing into the dining room where my sister and I were devouring breakfast. "And yes, I'll be casting Prudence Petty. She got a Best Actress nomination last time."

"If you give me a chance," our mother said, "maybe I could actually *win* Best Actress."

"Not this time, Lily," our father said, "but soon, okay?"

He reached out to pat her shoulder, but our mother shrugged his hand away.

"The show must go on, Lily," said our father.

Our mother turned and stormed away.

THE NEXT DAY, OUR mother suddenly "took ill," and in the weeks that followed she was rarely seen outside her bedroom, except to occasionally fetch a bottle of champagne from the refrigerator in the kitchen or a bottle of painkillers from the bathroom cabinet. The homeschool lessons that she normally provided for us were put on hiatus, and, with no play for the Fabulous Trouper Quintuplets to rehearse for or perform in, we went from our customary overscheduled lives to having almost nothing to do.

To keep us busy during the mornings, our father would pull down the movie screen in the basement of Trouper Terrace and thread into the projector the first reel of some classic film that we were to "study" to bolster our development as child actors: Judy Garland's performance in *The Wizard of Oz*, Shirley Temple in *The Little Princess*, Mickey Rooney and Elizabeth Taylor in *National Velvet*. Then he would scamper away to the Orpheum-Galaxie to direct and perform in the rehearsals for *The Cocktail Party*.

On one particularly rushed morning, as Joan, Violet, Olivia, Marigold, and I dutifully seated ourselves before the movie screen, our father loaded up a film and announced, "I've got a real treat for you this morning, children!" Then he switched on the projector and turned off the lights as he scrambled up the stairs.

My sisters and I waited in anticipation, listening to the slight *click-click-click-click-click* of the projector's sprockets, the whir of film reels turning, the subtle hiss of flowing film, and we watched the beam of light from the projector cutting through the air above our heads, creating little whirling galaxies of dust-fleck stars in its path. What could be better than *The Wizard of Oz*, or *The Little Princess*, or *National Velvet*, we wondered as the film leader onscreen began its countdown ... 5 ... 4 ... 3 ... 2 ... 1 ...

And then, before our eyes:

Joan, our father's biggest fan, clapped her hands and screeched, "Yaaaaaay!" Violet rolled her eyes and feigned a yawn. The rest of us merely sighed. We had already been forced to watch this film so many times before.

IT WAS AFTER WATCHING the excellent Thames documentaries *Unknown Chaplin* and *Buster Keaton: A Hard Act to Follow* that our father got the idea to make his own documentary, and although the title suggests that it is a documentary about the entire Trouper family, it's really all about him. The film might as well be called *Unknown John Lionel Trouper* or *John Lionel Trouper: A Hard Act to Follow*.

In the Charlie Chaplin and Buster Keaton biographies, our father loved the melodic-yet-authoritative quality of the BBC-English-accented narration, so he sought out a voice actor with exactly the same manner of articulation and tone of voice. When he could find no one who fit his exacting specifications (at least, no one who was willing to work for the pittance he offered to pay), John Lionel decided to do the job himself.

So, here is a little-known secret revealed: the off-camera character narrating the story in *The Troupers: The Show Must Go On*, that rich, authoritative, upper-class-English voice in the background posing all of the questions to John Lionel's mother, his wife, his children, and everyone else in the film, including John Lionel Trouper himself, is in fact John Lionel Trouper himself.

The credits at the end of the film look like this:

It's a testament to our father's supreme voice-acting skills that no one outside our family ever wondered who J.N. Loopier-Rhounlet might be or noticed that his name was a perfect anagram for John Lionel Trouper.

JOHN LIONEL TROUPER (V.O.)
(AS J.N. LOOPIER-RHOUNLET)
(dramatically)

John Lionel Trouper first enters the world in the year 1932. And on the silver screen, 1932 sees one of the greatest films ever produced make its audacious debut: *Grand Hotel*! Starring TWO members of the Royal Family of Acting … John and Lionel Barrymore!

PHOTO STILL: John and Lionel Barrymore, displayed on a split screen, their studio portraits facing each other in dramatic style.

JOHN LIONEL TROUPER (V.O.)
(AS J.N. LOOPIER-RHOUNLET)

And, into the Brave New World of 1932 is born … John Lionel Trouper!

DISSOLVE INTO — (PHOTO STILL): A photograph of baby John Lionel Trouper, positioned as if the previous portraits of John and Lionel Barrymore have merged together to create this saucer-eyed, potential-filled infant.

Dear viewer, did you manage to catch that subtlety? Our father was named after both John Barrymore and Lionel Barrymore, who starred in *Grand Hotel* together in 1932, the same incredible year that he was born! John Lionel Trouper was obviously destined for greatness as an actor, wasn't he? Did you manage to make that connection?

But wait! There's more!

JOHN LIONEL TROUPER (V.O.)
(AS J.N. LOOPIER-RHOUNLET)

But John Lionel Trouper's eventual success did not come without a lot of hard work, and he started out by working with and learning from many legends of the stage and screen, who took the promising young talent under their wings.

CUT TO — (PHOTO STILL): John Lionel Trouper poses onstage with legendary stage actor Robertson Addersley-Helm. Both men are in costume for their roles in a 1956 production of *Hamlet*, with John Lionel in the small role of Osric and Addersley-Helm as Hamlet.

I can't say for sure how much our father actually "worked

with and learned from" Robertson Addersley-Helm; the well-known stage actor was famously dismissive of other actors, so it's not likely that he voluntarily handed over much sage advice to our young father. Still, something of Addersley-Helm must have bled into John Lionel during their brief time performing together; in his obituary "tribute" to the legendary actor, famously acerbic reviewer Ethan Drake described Addersley-Helm's stage presence as "hammier than Easter dinner in the Black Forest," a line that Drake reused decades later in his review of our father's own portrayal of Hamlet.

JOHN LIONEL TROUPER (V.O.)
(AS J.N. LOOPIER-RHOUNLET)
Eventually, brimming with energy and talent, the young JOHN LIONEL TROUPER was ready to step into the enormous shoes of his legendary role models … and fill their shoes he did!

CUT TO – (STOCK FOOTAGE): A grainy, overexposed 8mm black-and-white film, circa 1959, of an animated, excited young John Lionel Trouper in front of the Universal Studios gates, posing and shaking hands with a distracted-looking Cary Grant and a jowly Alfred Hitchcock.

The juxtaposition of narrative and image is again misleading; it suggests that our father also "worked with and learned from" Cary Grant and Alfred Hitchcock, when in fact the two Hollywood legends just happened to be approaching the gates of Universal Studios together when young John Lionel sprinted from the tour bus he was riding in with his mother, enthusiastically accosting Grant and Hitchcock while his mother filmed their impromptu meeting through the bus window.

Neither Chrysanthemum nor John Lionel had come to Hollywood on official entertainment industry business; they were in California on vacation, and they had signed up for a fledgling version of the now-famous Universal Studios tour.

"UGH!" GROANED VIOLET. "I am not watching this again! I'm going outside to play. Who's coming with me?"

"I'll go!" I immediately responded.

"Me too," said Marigold.

"Me three," said Olivia.

"I love watching Daddy, and I love knowing his story," Joan said. "The rest of you can do what you want, but I'll stay here."

So, while Joan remained in the basement of Trouper Terrace, raptly basking in our father's obvious greatness once again, Violet, Olivia, Marigold, and I went outside to seek for ourselves a rare, unscripted adventure.

Scene 10:

The Honeycomb Hideout

(Or: Pop! Pop! Pop!)

DRESSED IN A SOLDIER'S outfit scavenged from the costume closet in the basement, it was Violet who led the charge away from Trouper Terrace. The sewn-on golden wings of Marigold's favourite angel costume flapped happily as she skipped along behind Violet, and behind her trudged Olivia, wearing practical boots and reasonable outdoor clothing.

I brought up the rear of our pint-sized brigade, constantly glancing over my shoulder, expecting our father to rush after us at any moment, to admonish us for breaking ranks, and to corral us back onto one of our stages to resume rehearsing lines and blocking scenes.

When we reached the drooping wire fence that marked the furthest limits of our grandmother's property, through the dense, shadowy forest on the other side, we could hear the Niagara River roaring.

"Come on!" yelped Violet as she vaulted over a low spot in the fence, waving like a sergeant at her siblings to follow.

Olivia, Marigold, and I hesitated at the fence line. We had never been this far away from Trouper Terrace without our father, our mother, or our grandmother, and we had certainly never left the grounds unescorted.

"Come on!" Violet beckoned us again as she scrambled down what seemed at the time to be a perilously steep and slippery hill. "I see something down there!"

Violet's three reluctant followers peered over the edge of the slope, and through the trees and brush we could see it, perched at the river's edge.

"It looks like a fairy's house!" Marigold exclaimed.

"Or a pirate's hut," I said, unsure of whether this would be a good or a bad thing.

"Or some criminal's hideout," Olivia grumbled warily.

As we watched Violet charging downhill toward the crumbling little building, the balance inside each of us shifted from fear to curiosity, and Marigold, and then Olivia, and then I stepped over the fallen wire of the fence and followed Violet down the hill toward the slanted, moss-covered shack.

Yellowed white paint flaked like dead skin from the lopsided old cabin, revealing a brownish-red wood stain underneath that looked eerily like dried blood. All of the windows had long been smashed out, and the scattered shards of glass were mostly covered now by dirt and fallen leaves. A slight gust of river breeze caused the warped wooden door to moan as it swung on rusty hinges, and the scent that emanated from inside carried hints of urine and animal feces and mould.

Olivia, Marigold, and I immediately tuned to flee back up the slope to Trouper Terrace, but as Violet stepped inside the shack, her delighted squeal caused the rest of us to turn back.

"Wow!" she called out. "Look at this!"

Inside the long-abandoned cabin, atop a splintered, dust-covered Formica countertop, someone had left an unopened twelve-pack of cola. Violet cheered, "Pop! Pop! Pop!" as she immediately tore the case open, cracking open a can and chugging it down. "Ohhhhh," she moaned ecstatically, "so gooooooooood!"

None of the Fabulous Trouper Quintuplets had ever tasted a soft drink before; sugary, carbonated, artificially flavoured beverages were prohibited with a maniacal fervour by our father. So, Olivia, Marigold, and I rushed inside to sample the forbidden elixir for ourselves.

Upon the warped countertop was also perched a small, battery-powered, pink plastic radio. Violet switched it on, and through its small speakers, music like we had never heard before blasted, voices harmonizing to a strong, synthesized beat, "POP! POP! POP MUSIC!" Then, as the song faded out, an announcer's voice brayed, "That was 'Pop Muzik' by M, and now here's the latest from Kenny Loggins ... from the hit movie *Footloose*, it's the song ... 'Footloose'!"

Soon the singer was wailing the chorus, "FOOTLOOSE! FOOTLOOSE!", and, fuelled by sugar and caffeine, the four wayward Trouper quints all danced together atop the creaky, uneven floorboards to the throbbing beat of this compelling, almost alien-sounding music.

Over the peeling, discoloured wallpaper, someone (probably some bored local teenager) had spray-painted words:

WELCOME
TO THE
HONEYCOMB HIDEOUT

None of us had any idea what this meant; because we had been barred from watching present-day television, we had never seen the famous commercials for Honeycomb cereal, nor would we have had any idea that certain teenagers of the day had co-opted the phrase to describe safe havens where they could hang out to drink beer and smoke marijuana, free from parental and legal interference. Nevertheless, some of the rebellious spirit of the Honeycomb Hideout seeped into us anyway.

Violet popped open her second can of cola and cheered, "This is *our* hideout now!"

We four rebels happily obeyed when a band called Prince and the Revolution instructed us through the radio's speakers, "LET'S GO CRAZY! LET'S GO CRAZY!", and we nearly caused the bouncy floor to collapse beneath us as another group, Van Halen, implored us to "JUMP! JUMP!"

It was then that Marigold noticed the stack of comic books tossed across the water-stained mattress of a half-collapsed bed. All of our eyes bulged wide. Comic books were also forbidden by our father.

Marigold picked up one called *Fairies and Wraiths*, with winged mythical creatures flying in bright primary colours across the cover. Violet grabbed one called *Jem and the Holograms vs. The Misfits*, which, judging by the cover art, appeared to be the story of two warring all-female pop bands. Olivia chose an issue of *Wonder Woman*, and I flipped open a copy of *Amazing Stories*.

If there had been enough time for any of us to actually read these forbidden tomes, surely we would have been corrupted forever by their subversive content, and anarchy would have overthrown the House of Trouper ...

But then the Wild Man appeared.

The first thing we heard were his knuckles rapping on the windowsill: POP! POP! POP!

Then we heard his monstrous voice.

"Who all's tresspassin' in mah home!" he roared in a terrifying accent somewhere between a Hollywood Nazi and a cartoon redneck drawl. "Ahm gonna cut y'all up and eat y'all for mah dinner!"

Then he poked his head in through one of the smashed-out windows, shaking his mane of matted hair and his shaggy beard, his face concealed by dirt and grime, his eyes bulging threateningly.

The cola cans hit the dirty floor, and we all ran screaming from the shack, tearing up the hill and over the fence and through the backyard into the safe confines of Trouper Terrace. We locked the door behind us and ran downstairs to the basement, where Joan was still raptly immersed in *The Troupers: The Show Must Go On*.

MANY YEARS WOULD PASS before Marigold and I would discover, stuffed inside a box in a backstage closet, the wig, false beard, and costume our father had worn that day. By that time, it was too late to change anything, anyway; the Fabulous Trouper Quintuplets would spend the next decade performing for our father without questioning or resisting any of his directions. Joan would do it because it was what she was born to do, but the rest of us would dutifully continue playing our roles because our father's uncredited performance as the Wild Man had made us terrified of the world beyond Trouper Terrace and the Orpheum-Galaxie Theatre.

But each of us, unknown to the others, had kept and hidden

away the comic books we found that day: Marigold had *Fairies and Wraiths*, Violet had *Jem and the Holograms vs. The Misfits*, Olivia had *Wonder Woman*, and I had *Amazing Stories*, each slim, subversive volume hidden beneath the mattresses of each of our beds.

Scene 11:

The Good Children

(Or: No One Likes a Tattletale)

DESPITE THE MODERATE SUCCESS of *The Cocktail Party*, our father missed the consistently packed houses — and the reliable income — of *The NEW Scallywags* shows, and so he hastily wrote the script for what he imagined to be a suitable replacement, a play called *The Good Children*. It consisted of several overwrought, on-the-nose, cautionary moralistic scenes, with subtitles such as "Lying Is Wrong," "Waste Not, Want Not," and "No One Likes a Tattletale," which my sisters and I dutifully performed for three long seasons of seven matinees a week, to the eye-rolling chagrin of the unfortunate youngsters who were forced to absorb our "lessons" and the great delight of the well-meaning parents and teachers who brought their children and students to the Orpheum-Galaxie by the busload. "Give the people what they want," our father would say, and in his estimation, "the people" were the ones who paid for the tickets.

My sisters and I were only five years old when we began playing *The NEW Scallywags* onstage, and our father directed us using methods similar to those of an animal trainer disciplining a litter of enthusiastic but rambunctious puppies; we were rewarded when we were "good," and we were punished when we were "bad," and as a result we all eventually became very good at playing our typecast roles. But now that he had added "playwright" to his illustrious theatrical resume, he wanted more from his offspring than "very good"; he wanted our performances to be perfect, for every audience and for every show.

SCENE: Upon the rehearsal stage at one end of the basement of Trouper Terrace, JOAN, VIOLET, OLIVIA, and MARIGOLD are running through a rehearsal for the scene entitled "No One Likes a Tattletale" from their father's play The Good Children.

The girls are cleaning up a mess together so their mother won't find out, when ERROL enters the scene.

ERROL. Hi, sisters. Hey, what are you four up to?

The girls all abruptly stop what they are doing.

JOAN. We're not telling *you.*

ERROL. Why not?

OLIVIA. Because you're a tattletale!

VIOLET. So leave us alone, tattletale.

MARIGOLD. We'll solve the problem without you.

ERROL. *(calling out loudly)* MOMMM! The girls are excluding me again!

JOAN. See? That's exactly why we're excluding you.

Ceremoniously, the FOUR SISTERS cross their arms tightly across their chests, and they simultaneously turn their backs on their BROTHER.

ERROL. Oh, please don't exclude me! I promise I won't be a tattletale anymore!

OLIVIA. *(without looking at him)* It's too late for that.

JOAN. *(head held high)* Nobody likes a tattletale.

ERROL turns and slinks away, tears in his eyes.

Offstage, from his seat in the centre of the basement, our father called to us, "Lovely, children. Lovely. That scene, overall, was quite good. However," he added, glancing at the stopwatch held in his left hand, "if we want this production to clock in at under an hour, we're going to have to spit those lines out a little bit faster. Understood?"

"Understood, Father," we all responded (except for Joan, who said "Daddy" instead of "Father").

"Oh, Joan, darling," he continued, "give me a little more dramatic flair on your final lines. Okay, dear? Really give it to Errol!"

"Yes, Daddy," Joan affirmed brightly, wriggling in place as if wagging an invisible tail.

"Violet, your final line can be a little more ... gruff. Olivia, you can be a bit more authoritative overall, I think, and Marigold ...

just a bit louder, sweetie. Your soft voice is getting lost back here, and there is a lot more space to fill inside the Orpheum-Galaxie."

Like puppies standing on their hind legs and barking for treats, my sisters responded in unison, "Yes, Father."

"And, Errol," the Great John Lionel Trouper intoned, "your character is in the wrong here. You understand that, right? You need to play the end of this scene with more humility ... with more meekness ... with more subservience."

Honestly, I was growing tired of always playing the character who had to be humble, meek, and subservient all the time, but despite not being the most natural performer of the Trouper Quintuplets, I nevertheless enjoyed being onstage with my sisters, and like them, I was also lifted by the applause that followed each of our shows together. Also, like the rest of my siblings, I still yearned for our father's approval, which he dangled before us like a trainer dangling fish before the seals at SeaWorld. There would eventually come a day when I would decide to bite the trainer's hand instead of jumping obediently for the fish, but this wasn't the day; I was only seven years old.

So, all I said in response to his criticism was, "Yes, Father" — humbly, meekly, and subserviently. I was John Lionel's trained pup, and, similar to the conditioned salivations of Pavlov's dogs, I responded almost automatically to our father's commands. When I didn't, it wasn't fun for anyone.

"Okay," our father barked, "let's work on the next scene: 'Waste Not, Want Not.'"

Joan, Violet, and Olivia went immediately into character and began acting out the scene, while Marigold and I, who didn't have any lines in the opening, stood inertly in the background. Marigold unconsciously began bouncing on her tiptoes, which caused the golden wings of her ubiquitous angel costume to flap up and down. When this caused me to giggle, Marigold began bouncing harder, causing her wings to flap like she was about to take off … which caused me to laugh even harder.

Our father halted the scene and hollered at me.

"Errol! You're out of character again. What is wrong with you!"

I stopped laughing. Marigold stopped bouncing.

"I'm sorry, Father," I said with maximum humility, meekness, and subservience. "It won't happen again."

"You're damned right it won't happen again!" our father bellowed. "Our dress rehearsal is tomorrow, Errol. Tomorrow. The show opens this Friday! Why do you think we're all working so hard? Everyone but you, that is."

"I'm sorry. I'll —"

John Lionel then turned to his four daughters. "Girls, your brother has let you down. Please turn your backs on him now."

Ceremoniously, Joan crossed her arms tightly across her chest and turned her back on me, as commanded. Violet, Olivia, and Marigold looked confused.

"Really?" Olivia gasped.

Violet wondered, "Isn't that just … a play thing?"

John Lionel lowered his baritone voice to its deepest tone, for maximum effect. "Girls, don't make me angry at you, too. Turn your backs on your brother now."

Violet shrugged and Olivia sighed, but they both reluctantly turned around.

Marigold did not, begging, "Daddy, wait! It's not Errol's fault."

"I got distracted," I pleaded. "I won't do it again."

"Well, you're right about that," our father rumbled, and he strode across the basement floor and mounted the rehearsal stage, grabbing me by the collar and towing me down from the stage, across the basement floor, and into his private office.

Inside his oak-panelled sanctuary, he dragged me past the wall covered with framed movie and theatre posters featuring his greatest performances, past the glass-windowed display cases that wouldn't look out of place in a king's library; artfully arranged inside the cases were several comic books and a board game featuring *The Scallywags* and a soup can and a box of soap flakes featuring John Lionel as a cherubic child actor. There were also dozens of photos of our father posing onstage with various co-stars, mostly young and almost exclusively female.

Our father then shoved me in front of the largest, most ornate display cabinet of them all, filled with the Great John Lionel Trouper's many trophies and awards, with each prize illuminated by a tiny overhead spotlight.

"Stay right here and ponder these for a moment," he commanded, then he retrieved some rags and a bottle of silver polish from a nearby closet and handed them to me.

I was sobbing at this point, but our father's stern face reflected in the glass over my shoulder didn't soften at all as he barked, "I didn't earn these awards by being distracted, Errol. I didn't earn them for falling out of character all the time."

Behind us, Marigold stepped timidly into the office, her voice almost a whisper. "Please don't punish Errol. It's not his fault. I was making him laugh."

Our father turned to Marigold, shrugged, and tossed a rag at her. "Then you can help him with his polishing, I suppose. Neither of you are to leave this room until every single one of these prizes is gleaming." Then, as he turned to make his grand exit, our father intoned, "This is for your own good, children. Greatness doesn't come in half measures."

When I was sure that our father was gone, I whispered to Marigold, "Do you think he's punishing me for something else?"

"What do you mean?"

"Well ... I think he wrote the 'No One Likes a Tattletale' scene about me. I think he thinks that I told Mother about ..."

Marigold's eyes widened. "Told her about what?"

I hesitated. "About ... what we saw."

"At the theatre?"

"Yeah. That."

Scene 12:

The Excursion

(Or: A Galaxy Far, Far Away)

A FEW WEEKS EARLIER, Marigold and I had been sent by our mother to the Orpheum-Galaxie to fetch our father for dinner. Although his revival of *The Cocktail Party* had been receiving rave reviews and earning respectable box office take, he had nevertheless taken to scheduling extra rehearsals on off nights to polish the dialogue and perfect the blocking. "Even perfection can be perfected," he boldly declared.

When we arrived at the theatre, the back entrance was unlocked, but when we went inside, the house and stage lights were turned off, and only the emergency lighting remained glowing. At first, we thought that our father had merely forgotten to lock up after departing the theatre ... but then we heard the noises backstage.

At first it sounded like an injured dog panting, and then two injured dogs. But soon it got louder, and eventually it sounded like two dogs fighting.

In the darkness backstage, it had been difficult to make out exactly what was happening, but we discovered that the noises were being made by our father and his co-star, Prudence Petty, who were entwined on the floorboards of the stage, rolling around like ... well, to our seven-year-old eyes, they looked like two dogs fighting.

Prudence had been the first to notice Marigold peeking through the stage right curtains.

"Marigold! Darling!" she'd cried out, leaping to her feet and smoothing down her skirt. "Your daddy and I were just rehearsing a scene for the play."

"It's a very intense scene," our father said as he also scrambled to his feet. "It needed some tightening."

"Your daddy likes things to be tight," Prudence said, winking at our father.

After glaring icily at Prudence, our father said to Marigold, in his distinctive Director's Voice, "Prudence and I are professionals, and we want to get our scenes together exactly right."

"Okay," Marigold said.

Then our father saw me standing in the shadows behind Marigold. He strode over to the curtains, reached through, and grabbed my arm.

"You will *not* say anything about this to your mother," he hissed. "She doesn't understand my artistic process."

All I could think of to say in response was, "Okay."

AS I CONTINUED POLISHING our father's trophies, I said to Marigold, "I didn't say anything to Mother. Did you?"

Marigold just shrugged.

"Do you think they were telling the truth?" I wondered. "That they were just rehearsing, I mean."

"Well," Marigold said, her lips arcing into an uncharacteristic frown, "I read the script for *The Cocktail Party*, and there is no fight scene between Edward Chamberlayne and Celia Coplestone."

"Should we say something to Mother, then?"

"No one likes a tattletale," said Marigold, and she set down her polishing cloth atop our father's ornately carved desk.

And that was the end of that. Or so I thought.

While I continued polishing, Marigold took the opportunity to snoop around our father's office, and soon enough she found something buried in the back of a file cabinet drawer.

"Ooh!" she said, brandishing a handwritten letter on frilly pink notepaper. "Listen to this!" Marigold changed her voice into what she presumed a Hollywood starlet to sound like — a cross between Eva Gabor and Katharine Hepburn — and began reading aloud.

To my darling John Lionel,

As you will know by now, I've just won my first Tony Award, and I just wanted to send you a quick note to say THANK YOU!

Without your guidance as my director during my time at the Orpheum-Galaxie, I never could have made it here!

With love and gratitude,
Priscilla Rappaport

From the depths of the same drawer, Marigold then plucked a signed publicity photo from the star of a contemporary TV show (that we had never been allowed to watch, of course). The printing at the bottom of the photo identified its subject as "Farah Nixon-Bluette, Star of NBC TV's *Sara's Insurrection*."

As Eva-Katharine Gabor-Hepburn, Marigold recited the inscription scribbled in black marker in the bottom right corner of the actress's eight-by-ten headshot.

To the charming and handsome John Lionel,

You are, and will always be, my favourite director!

With thanks for your wisdom and strength,

Your biggest fan,
Farah

"Hmm," Marigold mused in her own voice, "I wonder if Priscilla and Farah ever had to polish his trophies?"

I mimicked our father's baritone stage voice. "I didn't earn all of these awards by being distracted, Priscilla! I didn't earn them for falling out of character all the time, Farah!"

Then Marigold did her own impression of the Great John Lionel Trouper. "This is for your own good, Priscilla! Greatness doesn't come in half measures, Farah!"

Our laughter ended abruptly when we heard footsteps descending the stairs to the basement. I grabbed another trophy and began polishing it as Marigold tiptoed back over to the file cabinet.

But it was not our father who walked into the office; it was our mother.

"Hey," she said, "why aren't you two having lunch with the rest of your ..."

Her eyes darted over to Marigold, who was in the process of stuffing the note and photo back into their original slots at the rear of the drawer.

"What have you got there, Mari-Girl? Let me see."

With her eyes lowered, Marigold handed the note and signed photo to our mother.

As her eyes, beneath raised eyebrows, scanned the inscriptions, Marigold and I waited breathlessly for an eruption, but instead our mother just chuckled mirthlessly and muttered to herself, "Yeah, I used to feel that way about him, too." Then she handed both items back to Marigold and said parentally, "You really shouldn't be snooping around in your father's office like this, my loves."

As Marigold explained why we were in the office, sparks lit in our mother's eyes and threatened to burst into flame. Marigold's lower lip quivered, and she asked meekly, "Are you mad at us too, Mommy?"

Our mother knelt down before Marigold, her eyes softening. "No, no, Mari-Girl, I'm not angry at you. Never at you."

She stood up again and took Marigold's hand, then she turned to me and said, "Come on, Errol."

"But Father told me I had to —"

"It's okay, love," she said. "You are finished polishing trophies for today. And forever, in fact. So, follow me. Your mother has something more important for you to do instead."

Our mother led us up from the basement and out of Trouper Terrace to the carriage house, and she gestured toward the two-seat sports car that she had inherited from her own mother: a 1959 Renault Floride, the same kind of car that Grace Kelly drove when she first became the Princess of Monaco — but our mother's own flamboyant mother had one-upped Princess Grace by owning a convertible rather than a mere "everyday" coupe.

"Get in, my loves," our mother said. "We haven't got much time."

As Marigold and I squeezed together into the single passenger seat, our mother started the engine and slammed the transmission into reverse, then said, "There's a movie playing at the repertory theatre in town that I think you two should finally see."

"Was it made before the 1950s?" Marigold wondered as our mother backed the Floride out of the carriage house.

"No, it was made after, Mari-Girl. Many years after. It shares your birthday, as a matter of fact."

With stars in my eyes, I said the forbidden, mystic words aloud, "*Star Wars*?"

"*Star Wars*, my loves," our mother affirmed as she slammed the transmission into first gear and stomped the accelerator pedal. "*Star Wars*."

Marigold and I looked at each other, wearing identical expressions of excited disbelief.

Although we had led sheltered lives, sequestered inside the Orpheum-Galaxie Theatre, barricaded within the grounds of Trouper Terrace, barred from attending public school, and restricted to the consumption of popular culture created decades before our births, we were nevertheless acutely aware of the pop culture phenomenon called *Star Wars*.

We knew that it had been released on the same day that we were born and that our father held a weird, personal grudge against the film for upstaging the televised births of his own theatrical Dionne Quintuplets. We were only three years old when the sequel *The Empire Strikes Back* was released, but we definitely noticed the towering billboards for *Return of the Jedi*, which filled the movie theatres on our sixth birthday in 1983, the day of our last show as *The NEW Scallywags*. And we knew that it was the movie that every kid in the audience at the Orpheum-Galaxie had been talking about during intermission for months before that.

For our entire lives, every other box of cereal, can of soup, and package of pasta served in the Trouper household had flashed an advertisement for *Star Wars* and its sequels upon its label, raising the forbidden film to almost mythological status in our young minds.

Marigold's forehead then wrinkled with worry. "But what about The Rules?"

"I'm your mother, and I reserve the right to rescind The Rules as I see fit."

Emphatically, she slammed the transmission into second gear, and the Floride's tires bit into the crunchy driveway gravel as we surged away from Trouper Terrace.

TO SAY THAT MARIGOLD and I had never seen anything like *Star Wars* would be the understatement of the century; when it was first released in 1977, nobody else had ever seen anything like it, either. The film's awe-inspiring visuals resonated doubly with my sister and me, though, since the most advanced special effects we had ever seen in a film up to that point were the flying monkeys in *The Wizard of Oz*, which now seemed quaint compared to watching X-Wing fighters dodging laser-cannon blasts and racing through space to destroy the shadowy, malevolent Death Star.

"So," our mother asked us as we sipped on watery milkshakes and nibbled dry, overcooked hamburgers at one of the tourist-trap restaurants around the corner from the repertory theatre, "who was your favourite character, and what was your favourite scene?"

I had instantly related to Luke Skywalker, the farm boy trapped on a desert planet who yearns to escape and join the adventure of a space rebellion, but the character I really yearned to be was Han Solo, the roguish, cocky space pilot who shot first and asked questions later. I knew in my seven-year-old heart that I was no Han Solo, but I felt for the first time that maybe someday I could be.

"Han Solo!" I yelped in response to our mother's question. "And my favourite part was when he swoops in at the last minute in the *Millennium Falcon* to save Luke's X-Wing from getting blown away by Darth Vader's TIE fighter."

Because Marigold was so fond of cute, cuddly things, I half-expected her to claim the chirping, diminutive robot R2-D2 as her favourite character, or perhaps the huge, furry Wookie Chewbacca, but instead she cheered, "Princess Leia! And, oh, she had so many good scenes! Like the part when she tells Darth Vader's boss, 'I recognized your foul stench when I was brought aboard,' or when the boys show up to save her, and she says to Luke, 'Aren't you a little short for a Stormtrooper?', or when she grabs a gun from one of the boys and starts fighting the bad guys herself, or when ..."

Although it wouldn't manifest itself until many years later, in retrospect I'm not surprised that the feisty, strong-willed Princess Leia also left an influential mark on Marigold's psyche.

"So, Mommy," Marigold said, taking a slurp from her vaguely vanilla-flavoured milkshake, "what was your favourite character and scene?"

Our mother paused and considered the question seriously. "Although I also liked Princess Leia," she eventually said, "I would have to say that my favourite character was Obi-Wan Kenobi. And my favourite scene was the lightsaber duel between Obi-Wan and Darth Vader."

Marigold's eyes widened. "But Obi-Wan gets killed in that scene! The bad guy beats the good guy!"

"Yes," our mother said softly, "but did you notice that he glanced over at Luke and Leia before allowing himself to be struck down by the bad guy? By sacrificing himself, he was not only providing Luke and Leia with a chance to escape, but maybe he was also passing his powers on to the younger heroes so that they would have the strength to fight another day."

She looked seriously at Marigold for a moment, and then at me. "That's my interpretation, anyway."

LATER THAT NIGHT, MARIGOLD and I hid around the corner from our parents' bedroom, listening to the ensuing argument. We couldn't make out much of anything that was said behind the closed door, but we knew that many harsh words were being exchanged.

At that moment, I desperately wanted to be Han Solo, to kick my way in there with my laser-pistol blazing, and I'm sure that Marigold wanted to run right in there beside me as Princess Leia, but neither of us was ready yet to play those roles, so all we could do was listen in guilty passivity as the hours passed and the tide of the battle eventually turned.

Our mother's voice was inevitably drowned out by our father's, and eventually we didn't hear her at all. In real life, the good guys don't always win.

But maybe our mother sacrificed herself in order to allow Marigold and me to survive to fight another day.

That's my interpretation, anyway.

Scene 13:

The Scene

(Or: Like Blossoms Fallen from a Cherry Tree, But Also Like the Bits of an Exploded Grenade)

MY SISTERS AND I never really had the privilege of knowing the Ingrid-Bergman-meets-Grace-Kelly-meets-Barbara-Stanwyck-meets-Ava-Gardner version of our mother, who was described so gushingly in all of the five-star reviews of her performance in *Cat on a Hot Tin Roof*. By the time we were born, the fabulous, glamorous, ready-for-prime-time version of Lily Royale had already been replaced by a different character named Lily Royale-Trouper, our mother, our father's wife; and although she cared for us kindly, taught us diligently, and sometimes even summoned the courage to run interference between the director and us, even as small children we sensed that some integral part of her had gone missing, and as the years went by, the passion in our mother's performance had gradually diminished until there was almost nothing left.

Maybe, like so many other women, our mother suffered from

postpartum depression after we were born. Maybe she never managed to climb back out of it. Maybe the effect is five times worse with quintuplets. Maybe it's worse to the exponent five.

Maybe the dark times began for our mother when her parents died. My sisters and I were only infants when it happened, so we can't say for sure if this was the turning point. It has always seemed to me, though, that for a couple of nouveaux riches, theatre-owning, country club sophisticates like Herbert and Frances Royale, a hot-air balloon crash over the French Alps would be exactly the sort of elegant, exciting, exclusive way to die that they would have chosen for themselves; but I never really knew my maternal grandparents, and I'm sure that their only daughter could never see their demise in such a cavalier way.

Maybe Herbert and Frances Royale were the last remnants of their daughter's life before John Lionel. After they died, our mother was more or less trapped at Trouper Terrace with her husband's doting, overprotective mother; her husband's five tiny, needy, rambunctious children; and occasionally her husband himself, when he wasn't busy acting in, casting, producing, and directing plays in the theatre that her parents had once owned, the same theatre where she had once earned rave reviews for the only role she ever got to play onstage before being recast as a wife, mother, daughter-in-law, and homeschool teacher.

Maybe none of this resembled the future she had planned as the Ingrid-Bergman-meets-Grace-Kelly-meets-Barbara-Stanwyck-meets-Ava-Gardner version of herself. Maybe she woke up one day to discover that she had become irrelevant to her own existence.

Or maybe it was something else.

I still remember this one scene as if I am right in the middle of it.

Initially, it seemed like it was going to be one of the quieter afternoons in the lives of the Fabulous Trouper Quintuplets; my sisters and I were eight years old at the time, each of us absorbed in our own particular amusements atop the rehearsal stage in the basement of Trouper Terrace.

At centre stage, Joan was colouring with crayons in her treasured copy of *The Fashion Frenzy Colouring Book*, carefully shading in a slender cartoon model's ballroom gown in Sunset Orange and Atomic Tangerine. Upstage right, Violet was directing an elaborately plotted pistol duel between two khaki-coloured plastic army figures. Olivia was sitting in the upstage left corner reading a book called *The Junior Mathemagician*. Downstage right, Marigold and I were working together on a complex adult jigsaw puzzle: a picture of a sailing ship with elaborate rigging.

Marigold was wearing pigtails in her hair and was dressed in her angel outfit, its frilled crinoline and gold satin wings threadbare from her wearing it nearly every day for several years. Maybe that outfit gave her special powers, though, because I'm pretty sure that Marigold was the only one of us who even noticed when our mother slipped like a phantom down the stairs and into our father's private office at the other end of the basement.

All five of us immediately stopped playing, though, and watched with wide eyes when our mother burst through the office door again, red-faced, red-eyed, and screaming at the ceiling.

"If you're going to cheat on me, John Lionel …"

She shook a handful of eight-by-ten photographs above her head, which she then tore in half with a hissing rip.

"… don't do it inside the theatre with my family name on it. Do it — do them — somewhere else!"

As our mother continued tearing the photographs into smaller and smaller bits, our adrenalized father came running down the stairs.

"Lily!" John Lionel thundered. "What the hell are you making such a scene about! The children can hear you!"

"My family name is on that theatre!" our mother spit at him. "My fucking family name, John Lionel!"

Our father's voice became even more resonant. "Do not speak like that in front of the children, Lily."

"Sure. Right," our mother said, her voice trembling. "You're all about the children, aren't you, John Lionel? With a drawer full of pornographic pictures that any of them could find."

She hurled handfuls of the shredded photographs up into the air, and the bits fluttered down around her shoulders like New Year's Eve confetti.

Our father's eyes flitted to the open office door and then to the drawer that had been pulled out and tossed onto the floor, and the tone of his voice immediately softened. "Oh, Lily," he cooed, stepping gingerly toward her, "it's not what you think."

Our mother shook loose the bits that were caught in her hair, gesturing at the photographic shrapnel scattered around her like blossoms fallen from a cherry tree, but also like the bits of an exploded grenade.

From atop the rehearsal stage, all that my mesmerized sisters and I could do was to watch with wide, unblinking eyes.

"Lily, Lily ...," our father gently intoned, "those ... those were just ... artistic projects."

"Oh, I'm sure it was quite artistic," our mother said coolly. "You definitely have a way with the ladies, don't you, John Lionel? Believe me, I remember."

Our father moved again toward our mother, his palms raised in the air like a preacher.

"It's not what you think. It was an artistic project. Like Alfred Cheney Johnston used to do with the Ziegfeld Girls. It's not a big deal. Hell, my mother even posed for some nude portraits when she was with the Follies."

Then our grandmother's voice rasped from halfway down the staircase, "It's true, Lily. I did."

Our mother glared up at our grandmother. "You wouldn't have posed for these, Chrysanthemum. This is not art. This is pornography!"

Our grandmother stormed down to the bottom of the staircase, gasping, "My John Lionel would never! He would never!"

"Oh, but Chrysanthemum, your John Lionel did. What's her name again — that little blonde who played Celia in *The Cocktail Party*? Pretty Slutty?"

Despite our mother's damning accusations, our father managed to sound affronted by this. "Really, Lily. Her name is Prudence Petty."

It was at this point that Marigold cast an ominous glance at me, and, as so often happened between the two of us, I knew exactly what she was thinking.

Our grandmother crossed the floor toward our mother, speaking to her in a soothing but perhaps also slightly condescending tone. "John Lionel is an artist, Lily. You know that. He needs aesthetic diversions that help him focus his creative vision. And if he says that these photographs were artistic projects, well then —"

Our mother waved off our grandmother and turned back toward our father, whispering eerily, "She looks great naked,

John Lionel. She's got the same kind of figure that I used to have, doesn't she? Before the kids, I mean."

Our father put on a particularly pleading voice for his next lines. "Come on, Lily. They're just pictures. I won't do it again if you don't want me to, okay?"

"Wow, that's a grand gesture, all right," our mother said as she began pacing back and forth, the volume of her trembling voice rising. "My father's name is on that theatre, John Lionel. My mother's name ... Mom would die of embarrassment. She would just die."

Our grandmother spoke again in that practised matronly voice of hers. "Please calm down, Lily. I'm sure that there is a reasonable explanation for whatever you think —"

"Out of the way, Chrysanthemum," our mother barked, then she pushed past our grandmother and stormed up the stairs.

Then, halfway up, she stopped, turned around, and levelled a hateful stare at our father.

"Our name is on that theatre, John Lionel. It's all that's left of my family. It's all that's left of us."

Then her voice dropped to a whisper.

"It's maybe all that's left of me."

Then she turned and stormed the rest of the way up the stairs, while the rest of us — our father, our grandmother, Joan, Violet, Olivia, Marigold, and I — remained frozen in place, as still as statues.

LATER THAT NIGHT, WHEN Marigold was sure that everyone else was finally asleep, she snuck into my room, still wearing her angel costume with the gold satin wings. She gently poked my shoulder, whispering, "Help me put the puzzle together, Errol."

I knew that she wasn't talking about the picture of the sailing ship with the elaborate rigging.

We tiptoed downstairs to the basement, carefully skipping the creaky stairs and avoiding the tattletale squeals of the many loose floorboards of Trouper Terrace.

After an hour or so of gathering bits of the shredded photographs, Marigold and I began sorting the fragments and gradually piecing the pictures back together. The two of us had become quite skilled at completing jigsaw puzzles designed for adults — not children — and we soon discovered that the photographs from inside the desk drawer in our father's office were most definitely meant to be seen by adults — not children.

Marigold tore all of the bits into even smaller bits, and I scattered the pieces as far around the basement as possible so that the pictures could never be reassembled again. But those images would remain etched in my mind for a long time afterward, and probably in Marigold's mind, too.

Our father had a lock installed on his office door the very next day.

Scene 14:
The Drink
(Or: Naturally Effervescent)

INITIALLY, JOHN LIONEL TRIED to make light of, or simply ignore, his young wife's increasingly erratic and alarming behaviour. When she developed the habit of drinking two or three glasses of champagne at breakfast, then two or three more at lunch, followed by a full bottle of wine with dinner (with frequent "aperitifs" and "refreshments" between "meals"), her absentee husband could hardly protest, since her drinking habits were nearly identical to his own. Our father's own passionate, tumultuous, on-again, off-again relationship with alcohol had begun at a very early age.

In the present, soft drinks are produced pretty much exclusively by two massive global corporations who make billions of dollars selling their sugary, carbonated products. In the 1930s and 1940s, though, there were hundreds of local beverage bottlers, all competing to quench people's thirst for sweet, bubbly refreshment. In Niagara Falls alone, the general stores stocked not only brands that still exist today (Coca-Cola, PepsiCo., Hires Root Beer, Orange Crush, and Canada Dry Ginger Ale) but also a plethora of locally bottled beverages. There were at least a dozen brands of ginger ale (Royal Charger Dry, Niagara Dry, Festival Dry, Taylor's Dry, Robinson's Dry, Cotton Club Dry) and maybe a hundred different colas and artificially flavoured and -coloured "fruit" beverages.

Competition for sales was fierce, and bottling companies would try almost anything to get an edge on their competitors. So, in 1940, just as the popularity of *The Scallywags* was rising to its zenith (in France, Belgium, Holland, and particularly Canada) and the image of Scallywag Sparky was already being used to sell soup and soap, chewing gum and chocolate bars, comic books and board games, Chrysanthemum Trouper was approached by the representatives of several bottling companies who hoped to procure the rights to her son's likeness for use in their respective advertising campaigns.

(This scene is once again reconstructed theoretically, based on information gathered through reconnaissance missions undertaken by me and Marigold.)

In the sitting room of Trouper Terrace, two men sat across from Chrysanthemum and John Lionel. They wore identical pinstriped three-piece suits, and each held his hat politely in his lap.

"Ma'am, I'm Tobias Swill, owner and operator of the Swill Brothers Bottling Company, and this is my brother, Jacob Swill, co-owner and co-operator. Now, we know that you have been approached by other beverage companies who seek to use the likeness of your son, as Sparky, to promote their products, but we have a proposal that we believe you will find difficult to pass up."

Jacob Swill quietly nodded along with his brother's words, as if to affirm their truth.

"What sets us apart from other beverage makers is that our sodas contain all-natural ingredients. Our grape soda is coloured and flavoured with real grapes, not with unnatural additives and chemicals. And while other beverage manufacturers carbonate their beverages by pumping CO_2 into them, our grape soda gets its tickly, effervescent bubbles naturally!"

Chrysanthemum Trouper was horrified to discover that other soft drinks contained "unnatural additives and chemicals," and when she heard about the nefarious CO_2, she was already prepared to sign a deal. But she had learned much about business negotiations from her late husband, so she feigned a dubious expression and allowed Tobias Swill to continue with his sales pitch.

"Every bottle of our grape soda will feature a caricature of your son as Sparky from *The Scallywags*, and the soda itself will be called 'Scallywag Sparky's Grape Soda.' Not only will you and your son receive a generous signing fee, but you will also receive a royalty payment for every single Sparky's soda label that gets printed. We will also pay an additional royalty every time that your son's likeness is featured in a print advertisement or on any promotional sign or billboard. And, eventually, we will also hire him to play the voice of Sparky for our radio advertising."

Little John Lionel's eyes were wide and swimming; he *loved* grape soda! And his face on every bottle of grape soda that these men would make? And on ads, and signs, and ... billboards, too? And his voice on the radio?

"Say yes, Mummy!" John Lionel squealed. "Say yes!"

Chrysanthemum Trouper could never say no to her doe-eyed prince, so she regally declared to the Swill brothers, "My John Lionel will serve as the face of your product."

Before long, hundreds of children were slurping down bottles of Scallywag Sparky's Grape Soda. It didn't taste as sweet as NuGrape or Grape Crush, and sometimes the bottles exploded on the shelf without warning, but it was *All-Natural!* Sparky said so himself, right on the label: "All-Natural Effervescence! Made with REAL GRAPES!" And if this soda was good enough for the leader of *The Scallywags*, it was good enough for every other kid, too!

For a few weeks during the hot, dry summer of 1940, Scallywag Sparky's Grape Soda was outselling even Coca-Cola and Orange Crush in the corner stores of Niagara Falls (on the Canadian side, anyway), and it looked like the Swill Brothers Bottling Company would soon have enough money to produce their first radio advertisement, featuring John Lionel as the voice of Sparky.

Alas, the love affair with the new soft drink ended abruptly when hundreds of children began stumbling, slurring their words, and falling down as if they were drunk — because they *were* drunk.

There was nothing "soft" about this soft drink. The "All-Natural Effervescence!" created inside each bottle of Sparky's was caused by the fermentation of the juice from the "REAL GRAPES." Sparky's thirsty fans were guzzling down cheap, sweet sparkling wine as if it were cheap, sweet soda pop.

By the time the first newspaper was printed with the headline "SCALLYWAG SPARKY'S SODA SCANDAL," Tobias and Jacob Swill had already fled the country, never to be heard from again. All that remains now of the Swill Brothers Bottling Company are some empty, dust-filled bottles and a few rusty storefront ads featuring *The Scallywags*' Sparky, winking and saying "Made with REAL GRAPES!"; these curiosities still turn up from time to time at antique stores and garage sales.

Somehow, neither the filmmakers who produced *The Scallywags* nor John Lionel himself nor his mother ever faced any legal ramifications, criminal or civil, and the Scallywag Sparky's Soda Scandal story vanished from the newspapers almost as soon as it appeared, with Chrysanthemum Trouper insisting, once again, that no hush money was ever paid.

IN 1940, WHEN HIS mother negotiated the deal with the Swill Brothers, John Lionel was only eight years old. Whether it was because he enjoyed seeing the likeness of his face on every bottle or whether he actually enjoyed the taste of the product as much as he claimed to, the boy added a contractual demand that Tobias and Jacob Swill were more than happy to acquiesce to: a case of twenty-four bottles would be delivered to him weekly at Trouper Terrace. Young John Lionel loved drinking — or at least he loved to be *seen* drinking — a product that featured himself on the label, and the Swill Brothers certainly didn't mind the extra free live publicity.

After the Scallywag Sparky's Soda Scandal broke, and the Swill Brothers fled for parts unknown, their abandoned bottling factory was eventually sold by their creditors, and the remaining crates of the "grape soda" were shipped to the only customer who still had a standing order for the "naturally carbonated" beverage: John Lionel Trouper. Right under his mother's nose, the boy left handwritten instructions for the delivery drivers to stash the crates inside an old, unused livery stable at the back of the Trouper Terrace property.

As an eight-year-old, our father would sneak one or two bottles per day, and the buzz he felt from the cheap, bubbly wine merely amplified his sparkling charm as the rascally Sparky. By the time he was thirteen, though, he was drinking six to eight bottles a day, and it showed in his performances; Sparky now came across on film as clumsy, gluttonous, arrogant, and mean-spirited, and production of *The Scallywags* soon came to an abrupt and dramatic halt.

When Chrysanthemum Trouper finally allowed herself to see what had transformed her cute, charismatic little boy into a surly, oversized brat, she sent him away to the Young Star Rehabilitation Ranch in Beverly Hills, California, a facility that specialized in curbing the addictions of wayward former child stars.

Marigold and I were never able to piece together the story of the Rehab Era of our father's life because neither Chrysanthemum nor John Lionel ever talked about it, publicly or privately. No family photos exist from this time. There are no film clips. There are no board games, no comic books, no soup cans, no pop bottles featuring John Lionel's face. It's as if he simply disappeared.

But that wasn't the end of the Swill Brothers' influence on our family; like our father before us, it was Scallywag Sparky's "Naturally Effervescent" Grape Soda that caused each Trouper Quintuplet's own passionate, tumultuous, on-again, off-again relationship with alcohol to also begin at a very early age.

WE WERE SUPPOSED TO be rehearsing our lines for *The Good Children*, but since both our mother and our father had gone AWOL that day, and since our grandmother was sequestered in her suite smoking cigars and drinking bourbon, geometrically as far away from her grandchildren as the walls of Trouper Terrace would allow, my unsupervised sisters and I eventually climbed down from the rehearsal stage and began exploring the forbidden far corner of the basement, where a mysterious stack of sealed boxes and crates were stored.

Violet was the first to bail out on our rehearsal, grumbling, "Screw this" and leaping from the stage.

"Hey!" Joan protested. "We've got lines to run!"

Violet ignored Joan and began digging through the prohibited boxes, where she soon found something that was of interest to us all.

"Woah! Look at this!" she cried out, lifting the top from a dust-covered crate and holding aloft a bottle of grape soda featuring the smiling mug of our father as the cheeky-yet-cherubic Scallywag Sparky.

Violet then located a bottle opener in a nearby toolbox, popped the cap off, and took a swig. "Sweet and bubbly!" was her evaluation, and she chugged down the rest of the bottle of the Swill Brothers' infamous product, finishing with a reverberant, climactic burp.

Since we were still not allowed to drink soda pop, the rest of us immediately rushed from the stage to grab a bottle for ourselves, and then another, and soon we were feeling pretty grand.

Marigold began humming what sounded like an aria from an opera (I don't know whether it was one she had heard before or if she was just making it up), and then she commenced twirling across the basement floor on her tiptoes like a prima ballerina, her arms fluttering at her sides like a hummingbird and then floating grandly in the air like a hovering butterfly.

Meanwhile, Violet dug deeper into the forbidden stack of boxes, pulled out an old acoustic guitar, strapped it on, strummed an out-of-tune chord, and began hollering into a nonexistent microphone, "Thank you very much, New York! Thank you! We're the Misfits, and we love you!"

As if in diametric opposition to Violet's rock and roll fantasy, Joan climbed back onto the rehearsal stage and paced boldly back and forth, with one hand on her hip and the other cupped upward as if catching rain, crisply enunciating lines from Shakespeare: "Alas, poor Yorick, I knew him well" and "To be, or not to be, that is the question" and "The quality of mercy is not strained."

Olivia lay back on the cool basement floor, staring up at the exposed overhead joists and counting them aloud, "One ceiling joist! Two ceiling joists! Three ceiling joists! Ah-ha-ha-ha-ha!" She was mimicking the voice of the Count on *Sesame Street*, which we had seen once on a television playing inside a department store, until our father disapprovingly whisked us away, grumbling, "Don't watch that artless *tripe*!"

I just stood there, watching my sisters filling the echoing subterranean space with the huge sum of their combined personalities and enjoying the tingling feeling that was radiating outward from my belly and through my bloodstream, warming my body from the tips of my toes up, up, up to the arches of my eyebrows.

And, although I probably wouldn't have put it in these exact words at the time, I found myself wondering something like this: *Is this who we really are? Are we really the things that we are choosing to do right now? Are we the sum of the characters we've played, or are the roles merely subtracted from our true personalities? Is this who we really are?*

If the supposedly grown-up version of myself can't answer these questions now, then the eight-year-old version of myself surely couldn't.

So I just laughed.

We all laughed, at one another and with one another. Laughter echoed back at us from the stone-and-concrete walls of the basement, laughter like we had never shared before ... and never would again.

And so, on that afternoon in the basement of Trouper Terrace, each of the Fabulous Trouper Quintuplets, perhaps yearning for another taste of that elusive laughter, acquired a taste for alcohol that remains with us to this day: Violet and her Jack Daniel's with a beer chaser habit, Joan and her vodka martinis, Olivia and her single malt Scotch, me and my red wine.

Thankfully, none of us have ever been sent away to rehab because of our drinking habits.

If only our mother had been so lucky.

Scene 15:

The Incidents

(Or: Tokens of Appreciation)

LIKE OUR FATHER SO many years earlier, our mother's exile became inevitable as soon as her previously private drinking problem became a public concern, and it was Marigold who shouldered the burden of being the sole eyewitness to the first two of the three incidents.

IN THE YEARS THAT followed our *Star Wars* excursion, the quiet, dreamy Marigold began to subtly change, secretly embarking on clandestine missions that none of the rest of us Trouper Quintuplets would ever have dared. In the evenings after dinner, when we were all supposed to be sequestered in our respective bedrooms, reading scripts and memorizing lines, ruminating on our father's daily director's notes, or simply resting ourselves for the next day's performance, Marigold would climb up into the tallest tower of Trouper Terrace, where she could read, uninterrupted and unobserved, through a stack of recently released books that our father never would have approved: *The Handmaid's Tale* by Margaret

Atwood, *The Color Purple* by Alice Walker, *Beloved* by Toni Morrison, and dozens of similar titles.

Although the property was already becoming overgrown, and the neglected buildings had long since seen their glory days, the view from the central tower of our crumbling mansion home was still inspiring: one could see all the way past the Falls, over downtown Niagara Falls, to the whirlpool in the bend of the Niagara River, and sometimes all the way to the lake on a clear day. It was from the small observation deck at the top of this tower that Marigold witnessed Incident Number One.

On the morning after the first episode happened, I climbed up there with Marigold, the old spiral stars squeaking and moaning beneath our footsteps.

"It was like watching a montage of shots from a bunch of Alfred Hitchcock movies, Errol," she told me as we reached the creaky wooden crow's nest at the top of the tower. "Remember that overhead shot in *Vertigo*, where Jimmy Stewart's disoriented character is stumbling down the stairs of the bell tower? Well, that's what Mom looked like from up here as she tripped along the path to the carriage house ... it looked like she'd had quite a lot to drink. And that shot in *North by Northwest* where the camera is looking down from high up in the United Nations building as Cary Grant's character runs from the building?"

We leaned over the railing of the lookout, and Marigold pointed down to the stairs that led from the front porch of Trouper Terrace downhill to the carriage house.

"I felt just like that. I was too far away to have any effect on what happened next, and all I could do was watch as she drove away in the Floride with the top down. I called out to her, tried to get her to stop, to turn back, but she didn't hear me ... or maybe she didn't want to hear me."

My eyes followed Marigold's as her gaze drifted down along the gravel driveway and out onto the black ribbon of pavement that is the Niagara Parkway.

"At first, she seemed to be driving cautiously, and seeing her car slowly rounding the curves of the parkway from up here was like watching those aerial shots of Jimmy Stewart's car moving through the streets of San Francisco in *Vertigo* ... it was nerve-wracking."

Marigold's eyes surveyed further, past the Falls, along the river, to the bend where the whirlpool swirls and froths and churns deep beneath the jagged walls of the gorge.

"When she got past town, she started driving faster — a lot faster. I thought I could hear the tires screeching around the curves, but I was probably only imagining that. It reminded me of that scene in *Notorious* where Ingrid Bergman's character is driving drunk with the convertible top down, and her hair is blowing in her eyes, and she thinks she can't see because of *the fog* ..."

Marigold closed her eyes.

"And that's when her car jumped the curb, tore across the parkland along the river, and side-swiped the guardrail that runs along the edge of the gorge."

Marigold blinked twice, and her voice dropped to a near-whisper.

"She looked like a fragile stick figure as she stepped out of the car. And maybe my eyes were playing tricks on me — she was pretty far away from me then — but I swear she just stood there looking up at the sky, like she was Cary Grant waiting to be dive-bombed by that biplane in *North by Northwest*."

Marigold gazed out at the Niagara River in the distance.

"It was only a few minutes later that I saw the police cars, and the fire truck, and the ambulance, coming from all directions to converge at the point where her car hit the guardrail. Then

I heard the phone ring downstairs, and I watched our father and grandmother rush out to his car and roar away to the same place."

A breeze whistled up from the river, pushing back Marigold's hair. Then she turned and smiled at me, in a pained way that almost made me cry.

THAT SAME NIGHT, A tow truck was hired to bring our mother's inherited black convertible back to the carriage house at Trouper Terrace; amazingly, the little car was still drivable, and it suffered only cosmetic injuries in the accident. Our mother was also returned to us in similarly good physical condition, given the circumstances. Somehow, she was not taken to the hospital by the ambulance, nor were formal charges ever laid by the local police, yet our grandmother insisted afterward that none of her money had changed hands over the incident; the distance between Marigold's perch in the tower and the site of the accident was too great for her to know for sure if she had or hadn't witnessed Chrysanthemum Trouper removing her magical, problem-vanquishing chequebook from her ever-present purse.

The next day, instead of making an issue out of his wife's dangerous driving, our father tried to make light of the situation. During the high-speed finale of her inebriated riverside drive, our mother had knocked down at least one road sign with the passenger-side front bumper of the Floride, so our father made a great show of retrieving the rumpled sign that read "DANGEROUS CURVES AHEAD" from the roadside gravel and nailing it to their bedroom door.

Shortly after this sad attempt at flirtatious humour, Lily Trouper stopped sleeping with her husband altogether and moved herself into one of the many unoccupied rooms in Trouper Terrace.

Our father took down the bent black-on-yellow sign and stored it somewhere behind his locked office door.

WHEN SHE WITNESSED INCIDENT Number Two, Marigold was secretly breaking The Rules again by watching her current favourite movie, *Labyrinth*, for the third time.

As if her nightly sojourn to the tower to read forbidden books wasn't enough, on Thursday evenings, when the local public library was open late, Marigold would make her most daring and rebellious move: sneaking out of Trouper Terrace to make the trek on foot into town to return her secret cache of library books and exchange them for a half-dozen more. Marigold would also reserve one of the small viewing booths at the back of the library to watch one of their collection of contemporary movies on VHS tape, and she saw *Stand by Me*, *Ferris Bueller's Day Off*, *The Princess Bride*, and dozens of other late-1980s films that I never got to see until I was an adult and finally free from our father's film and TV viewing restrictions.

I'm glad that I didn't have to see what Marigold saw on that particular Thursday evening, though: our mother stumbling into the library, dressed in her transparent pink nightgown and nothing else, an empty champagne bottle swinging like a pendulum from her bony fingertips. On our mother's daily timeline, it was sometime between "wine o'clock" and "nightcap time."

Marigold switched off the TV, spun her chair around, and ducked down to avoid being seen, peeking stealthily over the sill of the viewing booth window. She removed the thick, padded headphones she'd been wearing just in time to hear our mother's slurred voice shout out at the stunned librarian behind the information desk.

"Have you got any booksh on shexual shelf-pleasure? Because

my hushband has certainly not been doing it for me lately!" Our mother wobbled atop bare feet and waved the empty bottle at the librarian. "But he's been doing it for priddy much everyone elsh!" Then she winked and whispered conspiratorially, "But we sistahs can do it for ourshelves, can't we? You know what I'm sayin', don't you, sistah?"

"Ma'am," the librarian said in a calm voice, "I'm going to have to ask you to leave."

Our affronted mother raged, "You're ashking me to leave? I pay my taxshes! It's because of my parentsh' generoshitty that this building even exshishts! I have as much right to be here as any —"

"Ma'am ... you're inebriated. Please don't make me call the police."

Marigold then observed in horror as our mother escalated the situation to the point that the librarian was, in fact, forced to call the police ... who immediately called our father, evidently, because John Lionel and Chrysanthemum Trouper arrived with them, riding along in the back of the police cruiser.

"Herbert and Frances Royale built thish place!" our mother cursed. "They built half thish goddamned town! I should have the key to thish fucking city! I should have..."

Her voice vanished as the two police officers escorted our thrashing, kicking mother from the library and into the back of the police cruiser outside.

As our father muttered something to the librarian about an "unexpected allergic reaction to prescription medication," Marigold watched our grandmother writing and then handing over a cheque to the librarian.

"Thank you for being so very accommodating in this difficult situation, my dear," Chrysanthemum Trouper said, flashing her

Ziegfeld Follies showgirl smile. "Please accept this gift as a small token of our appreciation."

Chrysanthemum Trouper later swore, of course, that none of her money had managed to find its way into the suddenly very accommodating librarian's bank account; but this time, Marigold had seen it happen.

Our father joined his mother in smiling broadly at the librarian like one of her kick-line colleagues. "Yes, thank you so very much," he practically sang in that charming baritone voice of his. "I'm confident that we will get these medication issues straightened out and that nothing like this will ever happen again."

And then, with his magic-cheque-writing mother on his arm, John Lionel made his way briskly toward the exit door of the library, his Cheshire smile continuing to radiate.

Scene 16:
The Cameo
(Or: Like a Rocket's Trail)

THE GREAT JOHN LIONEL Trouper took it all in stride when his wife's private problems with alcohol surfaced so glaringly in public; however, when our mother's erratic, champagne-fuelled behaviour appeared unexpectedly onstage — on *his* stage — well, that was another matter entirely.

SCENE: Onstage at the Trouper-Royale Orpheum-Galaxie Theatre, the first act of Cyrano de Bergerac *is playing out before a capacity crowd. The scene is set for the famous sword duel between the Vicomte de Valvert and the play's title character, Cyrano, performed by none other than JOHN LIONEL TROUPER.*

Although this is a serious adult play, meant to further the acting career of JOHN LIONEL TROUPER rather than the careers of his famous children, the fourteen-year-old TROUPER QUINTUPLETS are nevertheless being used as extras through-out the play; ostensibly, this is to add to their acting experience, but practically, it is because, unlike the unionized adult actors, they don't have to be paid by the play's producer, CHRYSANTHEMUM TROUPER.

Swords are drawn, and the duel will begin the moment after JOHN LIONEL TROUPER delivers his inciting lines…

JOHN LIONEL TROUPER. (as Cyrano de Bergerac) I dally awhile with you, dear jackal, and then, as I end the refrain —

JOHN LIONEL's lines are interrupted by a familiar voice.

LILY ROYALE-TROUPER. I understand that you've been dallying with at least two of your colleagues on this production, John Lionel.

LILY, who has snuck onstage through the stage right door, pushes her way through the crowd of actors playing townspeople, including her own children, THE TROUPER QUINTUPLETS. She is wearing her now-infamous transparent pink nightgown. There are shocked gasps both onstage and off.

From onstage, ERROL notices that his grandmother, CHRYSANTHEMUM TROUPER, has vacated her seat in the front row of the auditorium. He nudges his sister Marigold and points toward the now-empty seat.

MARIGOLD TROUPER. Uh-oh.

LILY ROYALE-TROUPER. (slurring her words slightly) You've got 'em paid off at the library and the polishe shtation, but I co-own this theatre, and I can come here any time I want to.

She raises her hand in the air for emphasis, spilling wine from the glass she clutches in her grip.

LILY ROYALE-TROUPER. Oopsie! Nobody slip on that, okay? Don't want our insurance premiums going up.

JOHN LIONEL does not break character, ignores LILY, and repeats the line that will start the duel.

JOHN LIONEL TROUPER. (as Cyrano de Bergerac) I dally awhile with you, dear jackal, and then, as I end the refrain … thrust home!

JOHN LIONEL (as Cyrano de Bergerac) lunges with his sword at the actor playing the Vicomte de Valvert, who, having no real alternative, parries and lunges right back at him.

Both actors must quickly redirect their weapons, though, as LILY ambles between them, facing JOHN LIONEL, who reacts slightly too late, tearing a small piece of fabric from LILY's nightgown with the tip of his sword.

LILY ROYALE-TROUPER. You've been thrusting it home even more than usual, haven't you, John Lionel?

LILY turns to PRUDENCE PETTY, who is playing ROXANE, the object of Cyrano's affections.

LILY ROYALE-TROUPER. He's been skewering you …

LILY turns to face AMBER ANDERSON, the actress playing THE DUENNA, Roxane's handmaiden.

LILY ROYALE-TROUPER. … and he's been dallying with you, too, hasn't he? *(cackling)* His sword cannot be stopped!

PRUDENCE and AMBER exchange icy looks, and then they both turn toward LILY.

LILY TROUPER. Oh, don't look so indignant, my darlings. I know everything that happens here.

LILY zeroes in on AMBER ANDERSON, who cowers.

LILY ROYALE-TROUPER. Don't worry, honey, you're safe… for now. I was once young and impressionable like you, too. Just don't do it again, okay?

As tears trickle from AMBER's eyes, LILY faces PRUDENCE again, and her eyes narrow.

LILY ROYALE-TROUPER. But YOU …

LILY hands her wine glass to the actor playing the Comte de Guiche, then grabs the dagger from his belt.

LILY ROYALE-TROUPER. This isn't going to happen again with YOU.

CHRYSANTHEMUM TROUPER bursts through the crowd of extras, and as LILY brandishes the dagger, CHYSANTHEMUM grabs her daughter-in-law's wrist from behind and wrestles her toward the stage right exit.

LILY ROYALE-TROUPER. (struggling as she is ushered offstage, shouting at PRUDENCE) You BITCH! You BITCH! (Then, as she is dragged past JOHN LIONEL) And YOU! You fucking BASTARD!

CHRYSANTHEMUM TROUPER. (gripping LILY firmly) There, there, my dear. There, there.

JOHN LIONEL TROUPER. (improvising while remaining in character as Cyrano de Bergerac) Adieu, madwoman, adieu. May the convent heal your troubled mind.

There is laughter and light applause from the out-of-towners in the audience, most of whom have never read nor seen Cyrano de Bergerac before.

The locals in the crowd, though, who are all too aware of LILY's recent eccentricities, whisper and mutter to one another, many of them sympathizing with JOHN LIONEL for having to put up with "that crazy woman."

Onstage, JOHN LIONEL raises his sword and makes eye contact with the actor playing the Vicomte de Valvert, giving him a moment to get back into character.

Their swords crash together, and the duel is on.

After our mother's uncredited cameo appearance, our father acted swiftly and decisively. Before the curtain opened on the next show at the Orpheum-Galaxie, our champagne-sedated mother was loaded into an unmarked white passenger van, which took her away to the Sunrise Mental Health and Addiction Recovery Colony.

We all stood at the top of the gravel driveway and watched as the van rumbled away from Trouper Terrace toward the highway out of town, leaving behind a thick plume of dust that hung in the humid air like a rocket's trail.

And then we all went back to the theatre, got into costume and into character, and played our supporting roles once again.

We didn't know how to do anything else.

Scene 17:

The Time Machine

(Or: An Auspicious Debut)

ALTHOUGH THE CALLS FROM the irate librarian, the local police, and the other "concerned citizens" abruptly stopped, the banishment of our mother from Trouper Terrace soon complicated things for our father in other ways.

Our grandmother flatly refused to oversee the homeschooling of her grandchildren. "How am I supposed to help them, John Lionel? I wouldn't even know where to begin." Then she added darkly, "Who knows how far behind they are? It's not as if that wife of yours taught them anything in ages."

Sadly, this accusation was true.

When we were little kids, our mother patiently and dutifully taught us reading, writing, and 'rithmetic from nine until noon every day, until it was time for us to either rehearse for or act in a matinee performance of *The NEW Scallywags* or *The Good Children.* When our lessons were finished each day, our mother would reward herself with a single lunchtime glass of champagne. By the time we were nine years old, though, our mother's daily alcohol intake had increased fivefold, and her interest in teaching us decreased proportionally. When the day arrived for our mother's stunning cameo appearance in *Cyrano de Bergerac*, we had more or less taught one another the entire grade eight curriculum without guidance from our mother or anyone else.

It helped that Olivia was a natural at science and mathematics and could explain fractions and decimals and integers like a pro. I was interested in history and geography and was willing to help my sisters learn enough to pass the government-mandated exams we were required to take each spring and fall. Violet was a natural athlete, and, like a frustrated drill sergeant, she grudgingly guided the rest of us through the officially sanctioned torments of the physical education curriculum. Marigold was a gifted artist who patiently taught the rest of us the techniques of drawing, painting, and sculpting; she also finished reading another novel every few days and thus became the human CliffsNotes for our assigned readings in English. And, finally, although Joan was certain that her charm and beauty would carry her smoothly through the ballroom dance of life, thus making education irrelevant in her case, she nevertheless acquired a propensity for speaking and reading *français*, a skill she shared with her *catastrophique* siblings with a certain air of superiority.

Since our grandmother was unwilling to take charge of the homeschool education of the Fabulous Trouper Quintuplets in our mother's absence, once again John Lionel acted swiftly and decisively: he pawned the responsibility for our schooling onto the teachers at Fallsview District High School.

And so it came to pass that, in September 1991, at the age of fourteen, instead of heading to the Orpheum-Galaxie for a rehearsal or a show, we Fabulous Trouper Quintuplets walked together to FDHS for the very first day of our formal education.

Because we had been exposed to almost no popular culture created after the 1950s, it probably looked to the other students like we had stepped out of a time machine from half a century in the past.

Most of the guys were dressed in variations of the same uniform: an oversized plaid flannel work shirt over a black T-shirt with a picture and/or slogan printed on the front, faded, frayed blue jeans, and sneakers or unlaced work boots. In my trim-fitting grey suit, I was trying to look like Cary Grant in *North by Northwest*, but to them I probably resembled one of the teachers: an ancient, out-of-touch, counting-the-days-until-retirement sort of teacher.

My fear was confirmed when a guy wearing a turned-backward Detroit Red Wings cap and an AC/DC T-shirt shouted out, "Hey, look! It's the new principal."

Another guy in a Red Hot Chili Peppers jersey countered, "No, it's David Bowie. The Thin White Duke."

A third kid, with shaggy hair hanging down the back of his Jesus Jones shirt, his chin sprouting six or seven fine black hairs, guffawed, "No, wait! It's Pee-wee Herman. Been to any good movies lately, Pee-wee?"

The three broke into fits of giggles over that comment, but I had no idea what they were talking about.

But it was even worse for my sisters.

Many of the girls at FDHS looked as if they were auditioning to be characters in *La Strada*, that strange Federico Fellini film about the circus. They wore metallic satin tights, thigh-high stockings, dangerously short skirts, and clingy, shiny tops that looked more like lingerie than school-day attire. They flaunted stripes, geometric prints, and neon-bright colours: electric blue and orange, fluorescent pink and purple, acid green and turquoise.

My heart raced, partly from the culture shock and partly for other reasons.

In contrast to the other girls beginning grade nine at FDHS, Joan wore a long black dress with a V-shaped neckline and a slit up one side of the skirt, the sort of dress that gives away nothing but suggests everything, like Joan Crawford's scene-stealing gown in *Grand Hotel*.

Violet, as if to distance herself philosophically from her least favourite sister, showed up wearing the athletic cleats, white soccer shorts, and T-shirt that she wore while kicking the ball around in the backyard at Trouper Terrace. With her short-cropped hair and her trademark steely expression, Violet resembled an androgynous version of Buster Keaton's misfit athlete character in the 1925 film *College*.

Marigold wore the same sort of flower-patterned dress that she had favoured since she was a toddler, but she'd added some eccentricity to her look by sewing the golden angel wings from her favourite childhood costume onto the backpack slung over her shoulder, reminding me of one of the fairies in Max Reinhardt's surreal 1935 film version of *A Midsummer Night's Dream*.

Even Olivia, in her simple back pants and conservative white blouse, managed to look out of place in this festival of big hair and exposed skin and electric-neon carnival colours, as if Katharine Hepburn had stepped out of *The Philadelphia Story* and into a Janet Jackson video.

As we walked into the school for the first time, we were approached by a girl with extra-high hair, wearing a short leather jacket with padded shoulders and a clingy, acid-green leopard-print skirt. She looked each one of us up and down and then declared, more to her compatriots than to us, "Umm ... Halloween isn't until next month, bitches."

Some other girls crept in closer.

"Let me guess ..." said the one wearing white tights, rainbow-striped leg warmers, and an oversized top with the words *COLOR ME BADD* printed upon it in bold letters. She pointed a long, sparkle-encrusted fingernail at Joan. "You're supposed to be Morticia from *The Addams Family*."

"Joan Crawford from *Grand Hotel*, actually," Joan sniffed.

"Say what?" Acid-Green Leopard-Print yelped.

Olivia was cornered by a third girl, whose rouge-outlined lips, dark eye shadow, and ringlets of blond hair made her look almost identical to the woman pictured on her oversized, neon-pink Madonna "Justify My Love" T-shirt. "So," she taunted Olivia, "you must be the winner of the Mizz Appelbaum look-alike contest, eh?"

We would eventually discover that Mizz Appelbaum was the school's ancient geography teacher, upon whose classroom walls still hung maps from when the Chinese cities of Chongqing and Beijing were known as Chunking and Peking, Sri Lanka was still the colony of Ceylon, and so on. Mizz Appelbaum apparently revised her wardrobe about as often as she updated her maps, and she had been wearing a variation of Olivia's outfit to school every day since joining the staff fresh out of teacher's college in 1959; she even wore the same style glasses.

Color Me Badd turned to Marigold and said, "And you? Are you, like, supposed to be Tinkerbell or some shit like that?"

Then another girl approached, wearing a completely different uniform: short, dyed-black hair, silver skull earrings, black jeans, black vinyl riding boots, and a black T-shirt with the words "ANARCHY NOW" printed upon it in white Gothic letters. She noticed the tears brimming in Marigold's eyes and said, "At least you're original. Unlike these Debbie Gibson clones."

"Shut it, Matilda," Neon-Pink Madonna grunted.

Matilda raised both of her black-nail-polished middle fingers in Neon-Pink Madonna's face.

Color Me Badd raised her voice. "Bugger off, you tubby sloth."

Matilda aimed her raised fingers at Color Me Badd and said, "Whatever, slut."

Color Me Badd took a step toward Matilda. "Ooh, you're gonna get slapped for that, bitch."

Violet stepped between them.

Color Me Badd lowered her hand. "Nice outfit, Pele. But soccer tryouts won't be until the spring."

Acid-Green Leopard-Print and Neon-Pink Madonna made a great show of laughing at that one.

"Oh," said Violet, continuing her stone-face Buster Keaton impression, "I thought soccer tryouts were *today*." And without waiting a beat for dramatic effect, Violet kicked Color Me Badd hard in the shins with her cleats, and as the blood soaked through the rainbow-striped leg warmers of her nemesis, Violet rasped, "Colour you *red*."

"You psycho!" her nemesis screeched. "You dyke-ass bitch!"

Violet took that as her cue to send the girl flying onto the freshly waxed tile floor with a perfectly executed shoulder check, then she spun around to face Acid-Green Leopard-Print and Neon-Pink Madonna. "Are you girls here to try out, too?"

They backed away.

And that was the moment when the actual new principal decided to emerge from behind his office door. He looked a bit like Glenn Ford in *Blackboard Jungle*, which I did not interpret as a good sign.

"Hey. Hey! Hey!" he hollered. "What is going on here? All of you, into my office right now."

It was indeed an auspicious debut for the Fabulous Trouper Quintuplets.

Scene 18:

The Young Star Theatre Development Program

(Or: All the Way to the Bank)

MY SISTERS AND I sat in a line atop the long wooden bench outside the principal's office, like prisoners awaiting conviction, while our father and the principal discussed our precarious positions as students at Fallsview District High School. Initially, both of their voices were loud and animated, making it easy for us to eavesdrop.

John Lionel could normally talk his way out of any sticky situation, but our father's eloquence met its match in the equally articulate new principal. Despite his many protests, our father was made to understand that his children would not be afforded any special treatment because we were "child stars," nor would we be granted any free passes due to our relative inexperience with formal education. In the principal's exact words, we would have to "shape up or ship out." He also made it very clear that, unlike the relaxed standards set by our mother, our high school teachers would actually expect us to finish homework and complete assignments and pass tests, and that those things would be considered higher priorities than rehearsing for and performing in plays for our father, regardless of how many Best Director awards he had won.

"Speaking of that topic," we heard our father say in his most reasonable and diplomatic tone of voice, "I have a proposal for you, sir, which may greatly elevate your status amongst the people of Niagara Falls during your tenure as the principal here. As you know, this town is all about entertainment, and frankly, if you want to maximize loyalty from the families you serve ..."

The volume of their voices dropped, and we were unable to overhear any more of the conversation. Time slowed to a crawl, and we could only wonder what sort of plea bargain our father was offering in hushed tones on our behalf.

When they finally emerged from the principal's office, both wearing serious expressions, the two men shook hands and nodded at each other.

"I trust that you will follow up right away on what we've discussed, Mr. Trouper," the new principal said sternly.

"Indeed, I will," our father said with equal solemnity. "In fact, the children and I will immediately have a family meeting to discuss the agreement we have reached."

Our father then led us out of the school, and we shuffled along behind him in a pensive gallows parade, around the block and up Clifton Hill to the Orpheum-Galaxie.

Inside the theatre, John Lionel climbed up onto the stage while we settled into five adjacent spots in the centre of the first row. As our father glared down at us in judgment, the old theatre's cramped velvet seats felt as comfortable as electric chairs.

As an adult, I learned by binge-watching family sitcoms on

Netflix that normal "family meetings" happen when parents and children gather around a dinner table or upon a couch in the rec room to discuss the pressing issues of the day. For the Trouper Quintuplets, our "family meetings" were more like being in the crowd at the Plaza de la Revolución in Havana, listening to Fidel Castro's amplified voice echoing from the surrounding buildings, or perhaps like Italians being bombarded by Benito Mussolini from that balcony in Rome.

Our father positioned himself at downstage centre, before the closed crimson curtain, the toes of his gleaming leather shoes poking out over the edge of the platform. He glowered down at my sisters and me as if the most violent storm of hellfire and brimstone was about to pour down upon us.

Joan looked up at him with glistening eyes, capitulating, seeking mercy. Marigold's lip quivered, as if she might burst into tears again. Olivia and I looked up expectantly. Violet, however, folded her arms across her chest and hardened her face into a mask of defiance, to convey the clear message that she was not at all sorry for what she'd done.

"Well, my children," came our frowning father's opening salvo, "I certainly didn't expect to be called into the principal's office on your very first day of school."

"Oh, Daddy!" Joan cried with her usual dramatic flair. "If you had been there, you would understand. Those awful girls! They ... they ..."

Tears dribbled from Marigold's eyes as she added, "We're sorry. We didn't mean to cause any trouble. We were just —"

"Don't be sorry, Marigold," Violet rasped. "We're not sorry. It's that snotty little clique of bitches who should be sorry, not us. If anything, it's them who should be —"

Joan then stepped on Violet's lines, blinking her big eyes and emoting, "You must be so disappointed in us, Daddy!"

"Disappointed?" our father said, his face suddenly breaking into a wide smile. "Hell, no, I'm not disappointed!"

Then John Lionel Trouper's Cheshire grin grew wider to show us all that his anger had been just acting, and the very finest acting, of course. He sat down atop the stage floor, kicking his feet over the edge like a little kid on a high swing.

"I'm proud of you kids," he continued. "I had to put on a good act for the principal, but ... come on! You're the Fabulous Trouper Quintuplets! You don't ever have to take any shit from those ... those rubes. Soon enough, they'll all be applauding for you."

Marigold and Joan's expressions brightened, and Violet unfolded her arms and placed them on the armrests of her theatre seat, but Olivia's face remained creased with concern.

"So," Olivia queried, "what did the principal say? Are we suspended? Expelled?"

"Aw, don't you worry," John Lionel chirped. "Your father took care of everything, like he always does."

Olivia remained dubious. "Oh? How so?"

"Well, Olivia, my doubting dear, I convinced the principal that we Troupers can provide something that his school doesn't have but desperately needs."

"Which is?"

We could almost hear a fanfare of trumpets as our father puffed up his chest and announced dramatically, "A drama program!"

My sisters and I took turns exchanging alarmed and doubtful looks with one another, then Violet finally said, "But that school doesn't have a proper auditorium."

Joan sniffed derisively and added, "That old concrete-block prison doesn't even have a stage in the gymnasium."

"And that," our father's voice boomed magnificently, "is why I have magnanimously offered the use of the Orpheum-Galaxie for that purpose. And the Trouper Family will generously fund the cost of each annual production. We're going to call it ..." (he paused for dramatic effect) "... the Trouper Young Star Theatre Development Program!"

Marigold leaned over and whispered in my ear, "He's naming it after the rehab clinic he was sent to as a teenager?" to which I whispered back, "We're not supposed to know about that, remember?"

Aloud to our father, Olivia wondered, "Umm, did Grandma Trouper agree to this?"

"She'll have to. You kids can't be homeschooled any longer, and, well, the deal is already done."

But Olivia was still not satisfied. "Does the school even have a drama teacher?"

And this was when our father rose to his feet atop the stage, basking in the glare of an imaginary spotlight, and declared, "As of today, my children, Fallsview District High School has a new extracurricular drama program, and, as the most qualified individual in town, I, John Lionel Trouper ..." (he took a bow) "... will be its director."

Joan cheered and applauded. Marigold smiled up at our father, but then raised one skeptical eyebrow at me. Violet and Olivia exchanged side-eyed glances as our father continued his monologue.

"The principal will make an announcement next week, and we will hold auditions here at the theatre immediately after school hours."

It was now Joan's turn to look concerned. "Will we be allowed to audition, Daddy?"

"Obviously!" our father chortled. "You are, without question, the five best actors at that school, so the five top roles will automatically go to you."

Violet cocked her head sideways. "Umm ... don't you think that will upset the other kids who show up to audition? Not to mention their parents."

"Of course not!" our father brayed. "They'll thank us just for the opportunity to be seen upon this marvellous stage, inside this landmark theatre. They will be eternally grateful to work with a director of my calibre. And they will be overjoyed to learn the craft by working alongside professionals like yourselves. You were *The NEW Scallywags*! You were *The Good Children*! And soon you'll be the five most popular kids at Fallsview High."

But Olivia remained unconvinced. "Are ... you sure about this?"

"I am more than sure about it. We'll put on plays with huge supporting casts, with plenty of extras in the background. We'll give every kid at the school a little one-line role if they want one. And then ..."

The Great John Lionel Trouper stopped abruptly and gazed out into the empty seats in the Orpheum-Galaxie, above the heads of the Fabulous Trouper Quintuplets, up into the balcony and beyond, his voice rising gradually to a dramatic crescendo.

"And then we will sell tickets to every kid's family ... their parents, grandparents, aunts, uncles, siblings, cousins ... we'll have full houses for weeks. It will be their little darlings' brief but glorious five minutes of fame. They'll proudly snap pictures of their little human props. They'll applaud and cheer for their inanimate little spurts."

Then he pressed his fingertips together beneath his chin in a consciously diabolical way.

"And the Troupers ... will laugh ... all the way ... to the bank."

Scene 19:

The Audition

(Or: Shimmy, Shimmy, Shake It!)

IT IS AT THIS point in the story that our father finally found an excuse to transform his offspring into something more closely resembling his original dream, and the Fabulous Trouper Quintuplets finally became the Fabulous Trouper Sisters. It happened like this …

Our father stood at the foot of the stage, dressed in what had become his official director's uniform: a navy blue double-breasted suit with polished brass buttons, French cuffs on his ivory shirt, and a golden cravat tucked perfectly into his tall shirt collar. He believed that this costume projected both his talent and his authority: the perfect blend of Alfred Hitchcock at the height of his career and Steven Spielberg at Cannes, with a dash of Clark Gable in *Gone with the Wind*.

I was standing onstage at the Orpheum-Galaxie, "auditioning" for the Trouper Young Star production of *Toad of Toad Hall*, and although there was the implicit understanding that the role of Mr. Toad was already mine, I was nevertheless giving the audition my best effort anyway, to prove to the other potential actors in the auditorium that I deserved the role, that it was not simply being given to me. Also — if I'm going to be completely honest about it — practically everyone who showed up to audition that day was female, and perhaps I was hamming up my performance just a little bit for them; maybe I had a few of the Great John Lionel Trouper's genes in me after all.

Our father paced back and forth before the stage, holding a clipboard in one hand and speaking with the upper-class English accent that he usually reserved for speaking at awards ceremonies and playing actual Englishmen. "Errol, let's run that scene again," he intoned. "Your dialogue delivery was fine, but your singing was a bit pitchy throughout the song."

I glanced down dubiously at my sisters, who were all seated in the front row. Violet, Olivia, and Marigold all shook their heads. Joan merely shrugged her shoulders; it was never her place to disagree with the director.

Flabbergasted, I blurted, "Where, exactly, was I pitchy, Dad?"

The director sniffed and grandly straightened his cravat. "I am not your father right now, Errol. I am your director. In this situation, you may refer to me as Mr. Director or, less formally, as sir."

Our father then glanced around at the eager faces filling the auditorium, whose eyes were all fixed upon him, and he smiled benevolently; his grandstanding was having the desired effect on the masses.

At the same moment, I caught the eye of one particularly cute young woman in the audience, who was wearing a red French beret and fifties-style cat-eye glasses, and a strange, rebellious feeling filled my chest.

"Yes, sir," I said curtly. "My profuse and profound apologies, sir." Then I clicked my heels together and saluted, which caused Red Beret and several other girls to giggle.

Our father turned toward the source of the giggling. "Please, ladies, no talking during auditions. I understand that you are excited and eager to show us your obvious talents onstage, but please afford others the same attention and consideration that you will want when it's your turn to shine."

Then he smiled and winked at the gigglers in a way that was not entirely fatherly or directorial, and they beamed back at him, starry-eyed. Our father may have been nearly sixty years old, and these potential actresses may have been nearly the same age as his own daughters, but he seemed unable to stop himself from flirting with anyone equipped with two x chromosomes.

The director then turned to face me, with a slightly sour look on his face. "Now, according to my notes, you were a bit sharp on the high notes and slightly flat on the last line of the song. Let's try it again ... but in key this time."

I caught the eye of Red Beret again, and, sounding more defiant than I'd meant to, I responded, "I wasn't sharp or flat anywhere, sir. I sang every note of that song in key." Then I added another "Sir."

The director's eyes narrowed. "Are you questioning my ability to discern pitch?"

I hesitated before dropping the bomb.

"Well, yes, sir," I said. "I've heard your single. Sir."

The mouths of all the Trouper sisters dropped open; none of them could believe that I'd had the audacity to mention ... The Single.

WHEN OUR FATHER EMERGED in the 1950s after lying low for a while following his rehab stint at the Young Star Rehabilitation Ranch, rock and roll was taking over the world, and when John Lionel heard Elvis Presley singing "Hound Dog" and "Don't Be Cruel" on radio stations everywhere, he knew that he had found his future calling. He convinced his doting mother to invest in a recording session at a local Niagara Falls studio, which produced a 45 rpm single of "Rockin' J.L. Trouper" singing a song he wrote himself, called "Shimmy, Shimmy, Shake It!"

The song went like this:

Shimmy, shimmy, shake it, baby
Shake it for me
Shimmy, shimmy, shake it, baby
Yes, yes, sir-ree!
Shimmy, shimmy, shake it, baby
Gimme somethin' to see!
Shimmy, shimmy, shimmy, shimmy,
Shake it, shake it, baby
For meeeeeeeeee!

(Repeat *ad nauseam*)

The single was heard a few times on Niagara's local radio station, courtesy of our grandmother buying commercial time for the song to be played, and the record sold exactly one hundred copies in North America, which Chrysanthemum Trouper herself purchased directly from the recording studio; the crate full of unopened 45s is still stored in the basement of Trouper Terrace.

Despite the song's insightful lyrics and powerful philosophical undertones, the mass appeal of "Shimmy, Shimmy, Shake It!" may have been limited by our father's five-note vocal range, and perhaps also by his inability to sing in key. The best studio musicians that money could buy, combined with all of the reverb effect in the world, couldn't salvage John Lionel's warbling, hopelessly tone-deaf vocal performance.

Nevertheless, at the time our father was fond of telling his teenaged conquests that his "hit song" had made it all the way to Number 3 on the charts, but he neglected to mention that it was on the "Comedy Recordings" chart ... in Belgium, where *The Scallywags* was enjoying an unprecedented comeback on one of the country's fledgling television stations, and where the single was marketed as a novelty item, labelled "Scallywag Sparky Chante une Chanson Rock 'n' Roll!"

Whenever a potential girlfriend asked to listen to the actual song, though, the jig was up, and young John Lionel soon realized that he would have more future romantic success as an actor than a singer. So, he returned to the stage, and his one-song recording career was never mentioned again ... until, as young children, my sisters and I discovered the crate full of never-played records.

It was the same day we happened upon the leftover case of Scallywag Sparky's "Naturally Effervescent" Grape Soda that we found the 45s, hidden deep inside the pile of boxes in a corner of the basement, obscured by piles of scripts and playbills and old publicity photos of our father.

"Oh ... my ... freakin' ... GAWD!" Violet gasped as she tugged one of the records from the crate, slipped it from its paper sleeve, and dropped it onto the platter of our plastic Mickey Mouse record player.

We were already feeling giddy from the effects of the Swill Brothers' inadvertently inebriating soda, and hearing our father's screechy, overwrought rendition of "Shimmy, Shimmy, Shake It!"

elevated our already delirious laughter to maniacal, breathless howling. So outrageously bad was the song, and so boisterous was our reaction to it, that we didn't hear our father's footsteps descending the stairs.

As he towered over us, he said nothing about the fact that we were obviously under the influence of alcohol, but he definitely expressed his displeasure at finding us literally rolling on the floor in conniptions of laughter over "Shimmy, Shimmy, Shake It!"

He snatched the record from the turntable and snapped it in half.

Then he hurled our Mickey Mouse record player against a nearby wall. Mickey's left arm, the one with the phonograph needle built into his pointer finger, was severed in the crash.

Then our father pointed his own finger at the rehearsal stage and said, "Now get yourselves back onstage, and don't stop rehearsing until I tell you to stop."

And then he stormed back up the stairs and didn't return until late that evening.

And so, from that moment forward, in addition to being banned from watching any films or TV shows created after the 1950s, the Fabulous Trouper Quintuplets were also unable to listen to any records from any artist or time period. The remainder of our collective childhood would be without music, all because of one otherwise unheard song.

SO MANY YEARS LATER, it appeared that our father was still embarrassed by the single. It was too late for me to backpedal, so I decided to double down on my daring gamble, and from my position onstage I began singing, "Shimmy, shimmy, shake it, baby, shake it for me ..."

Our father's face flushed red, and he stammered, "You … you ungrateful little … get off my stage! Get out of my theatre!"

I folded my arms across my chest and stood tall.

Trembling with rage, our father crisply enunciated each word: "Get. Off. My. Stage."

"Okay," I said with a shrug as I stepped down from the stage. "But I wasn't singing out of key."

As I sat down beside my mortified sisters, the Great John Lionel Trouper took a moment to compose himself, masking his hateful scowl with a veneer of authoritative charm. Then he turned around to face the auditorium full of hopeful wannabe starlets, lowered his baritone voice several notes, and read the name of the next (and only other) male actor on the call sheet.

Before the nervous, sweating boy even had a chance to read a single line, the director declared boldly, "I don't even need to hear you read, son! I can tell just by looking that you are perfect for the role of Mr. Toad!"

The freshly appointed Mr. Toad stammered, "Umm … I … I can't actually sing. At all."

"Not a problem, son!" brayed our father. "You can speak the singing parts instead. No big deal. Congratulations, son!

Yes, our father called my replacement "son." Three times. No big deal.

As the auditions continued onstage, Marigold leaned over and whispered in my ear, "Don't let this get you down."

"I wasn't singing out of key."

"I know. And so does he."

Scene 20:

The Amazing Adventures of Errol Trouper

(Or: Free Time)

MY EXILE FROM THE Fabulous Trouper Quintuplets was the main topic of discussion at Trouper Terrace that evening.

"You can't just fire your own son," Olivia protested.

"But I *can* refuse to cast an actor who turns in a subpar audition," our father answered coolly. "And that is what I did."

Joan looked at our father and no one else, blinking her eyes like a Kewpie doll. "That seems fair to me, Daddy."

Violet sneered and whispered, "Kiss-ass," then raised her voice and demanded, "So, if I don't agree with something you say, are you going to fire me, too? Because if that's the way it's going to be, then I might as well step down right now."

"Disagreeing with the director is one thing," our father said evenly, his eyes darting in my direction. "Disrespecting the director is another."

Our grandmother then contributed a rare, raspy note to the

conversation. "Well, John Lionel," she wheezed, pausing to take a sip from her bourbon snifter, "I seem to recall that you had a fair amount of lip for the director, the producer, the camera operator, the cast, and just about everyone else involved in the production of *The Scallywags* ... and no one fired you."

"I was the star of that show," John Lionel barked. "Without me, there would have been no *Scallywags*."

Before speaking again, our grandmother studied the swirl of dark, fragrant bourbon circling the bowl of her glass. "Hmm ... *The Scallywags* would have been impossible without whom? I seem to recall that there was a particular executive producer who underwrote all of the expenses for that production, and without whom ..." She paused to take a long, slow sip of her drink. "... without whom there would certainly have been no *Scallywags* ... and perhaps no John Lionel Trouper, either."

After gazing at his elderly mother for a moment, our father finally said, "Everyone relax, okay? Errol hasn't been fired. He merely didn't make the cut for a role in this particular production. And this is not to say that he won't be perfect for a role in our next play. In the meantime, I'm going to make him the assistant director for *Toad of Toad Hall*." He finally looked at me. "Is that okay with you, Errol?"

"Yes, sir." What else could I say?

He said "assistant director" to my sisters and grandmother, but what the master of semantics really meant was that I would be the "director's assistant." I would iron and repair costumes, I would polish shoes, I would sweep and mop the stage before and after each rehearsal and performance. I would fetch hot coffee and cold drinks and pens and paper and whatever else the director decided he needed or wanted at any particular moment. Whenever our father caught me having a conversation with one of the young actresses in the cast, he would immediately send me away on some trivial and demeaning mission: "The green room toilet is plugged again, Errol" or "Go fetch me another cup of coffee, Errol — and wash my mug, for gawd's sake. It's filthy."

As much as I wanted to quit, to just walk away from the Orpheum-Galaxie and never come back, I also knew that this was what the Great John Lionel Trouper wanted me to do, and I would not give him that pleasure. I did everything he asked while wearing a subservient-yet-subversive smile, and I never responded with anything more than "Yes, sir" or "No, sir." I would fetch, I would mend, and I would clean, and when audition time came around for the next production of the Trouper Young Star Theatre Program, I would rise to the occasion. I would deliver the most perfect line readings in the history of the theatre, and I would be back in the spotlight with my sisters again.

But I was wrong.

Other than the character of Mr. Toad himself, John Lionel cast *Toad of Toad Hall* entirely with female actors, and he discovered during rehearsals that he very much enjoyed directing young actresses who were not his daughters. He was immediately enamoured of the sprightly, enthusiastic energy that these beginners displayed as they pranced and hopped and scurried around onstage as the anthropomorphized forest animal characters of the play. John Lionel gleefully controlled the entire ballet, shouting, "More movement, ladies! More energy! Slinkier! Sexier! More! More! More!"

So, I suppose I shouldn't have been surprised when the scripts that our father chose for the next three seasons of the Trouper Young Star Theatre Program were *Steel Magnolias*, *Nunsense*, and *The Women* — plays with all-female casts. It was with this announcement that John Lionel's vengeance upon his only son for the crime of mentioning The Single was exacted: I would not get a chance to act again at the Orpheum-Galaxie for at least three seasons. I had been officially exiled from the stage.

And his vengeance didn't end there: at the end of the run of *Toad of Toad Hall*, the Great John Lionel Trouper cornered me backstage, informing me succinctly that he "did not enjoy or appreciate" my "selfish, attention-seeking attitude," which I interpreted to mean that he didn't like it when I talked to the members of his all-female cast backstage. "You are an unwelcome distraction to my actresses," he railed. "They need to focus all of their energy and attention on the *play*." Which meant *him*, of course. Our father concluded his rant with an ultimatum: I could either perform my duties as assistant director "punctually, diligently, respectfully, and silently" or I could "find something else to do."

It was at that moment that I finally understood. As a child, I had tried to be obedient and capitulating, to play each role exactly the way he directed me to play it, to deliver each line as per his exact instructions, but that wasn't what he wanted. As a teenager, I'd been trying to show him the sort of personality and individualism that he seemed to admire in my sisters, but that wasn't what he desired, either.

But now I finally knew what he wanted from me. So I gave it to him.

"Okay," I said. "I'll find something else to do."

AND SURRENDERING TO OUR father turned out to be the best thing I ever could have done for myself. While Joan, Violet, Olivia, and Marigold toiled away their after-school hours onstage at the Orpheum-Galaxie, memorizing lines, blocking scenes, being fitted for costumes, participating in dialogue drills and dress rehearsals, I experienced for the first time a phenomenon that none of the Trouper Quintuplets had ever known: free time.

I used small rations of my new and precious free time to rework the short stories I had written in my Writer's Craft class. When our teacher leaned over my desk to tell me, almost secretively, that my work had a lot of promise and that with a bit of revising and polishing I could be the next F. Scott Fitzgerald, I got right down to business revising and polishing.

I measured out a few more portions of my free time to take an after-school driver education course; I enrolled on the day I turned sixteen, while my sisters spent their collective sweet sixteenth birthday onstage, performing their roles in *Steel Magnolias*. My sisters earned standing ovations, and I earned my beginner's-level driver's licence. As always, Grandma Trouper funded the production costs of the play, but she also paid for an auto insurance policy for me so I could practise driving in our mother's dormant, battle-scarred 1959 Renault Floride. As Chrysanthemum autographed the cheque (almost automatically), she winked at me and said, "What your father doesn't know won't hurt him."

I invested the remainder of my free time with some new friends, mostly girls from school who seemed to like my offbeat fashion sense and the fact that I now drove a vintage convertible. Sometimes we even got together during hours that were not technically free time at all; our grandmother's habit of smiling sweetly and signing anything put in front of her was useful whenever I wanted to play hooky with one of my new friends. I would write a note excusing myself from my classes, and then our grandmother would bestow her swirling, old-school signature at the bottom of the page. Since she was the sole financial supporter of FDHS's

Young Star Theatre Development Program, and also because she had made magnanimous formal donations to the FDHS Athletic Fund and the Scholarship Fund, the principal was inclined to accept any other documents bearing Chrysanthemum Trouper's signature without question.

So, thanks to our former-showgirl grandmother, my offstage adventures with my new friends were frequent and free. We did all of the things that tourists do in Niagara Falls, none of which I had ever done before.

On an adventure with one of my new friends, we boarded the *Maid of the Mist*, and despite wearing the hooded, blue plastic garbage bags they issued when we bought our tickets, we got soaked to our skins next to the Falls' churning downpour, laughing the whole time.

Another new friend and I climbed down the steep, rocky walls of the Niagara River gorge, holding each other's hands to prevent ourselves from falling, and then we sat at the river's edge and watched the currents colliding in the Whirlpool Rapids.

I rode the elevator up to the top of the Skylon Tower with another new friend, and we found both Trouper Terrace and the Orpheum-Galaxie from high up above. Then we posed with wax facsimiles of Madonna and James Dean and Elvis Presley and Marilyn Monroe at the wax museum, and then simultaneously laughed and screamed at the threadbare Wolfman and glowing-red-eyed Dracula automatons who lurched out at us inside the haunted house.

Another new friend and I pushed our way into the crowds at Table Rock to watch the fireworks overhead and the coloured lights projected onto the Falls. Then we walked through the garish midnight neon glare of Clifton Hill, pretending that we were Frank Sinatra and Ava Gardner, about to skip the line to meet up with Dean Martin and Sammy Davis, Jr. inside some posh club in Vegas.

After a movie date with another new friend, we raced along the highway in the Floride, passing other cars like they were standing still, then we squealed around the curves of two-lane blacktop that ran alongside the steep cliffs of the Niagara River gorge. The top was down, and the wind whipped our hair around and made our eyes water, and she screamed with joy at the speed and the sound and the danger; it reminded me of that scene with Cary Grant and Ingrid Bergman in *Notorious*. Then I recalled the part of the film when Cary Grant rubs noses with her, presses his cheek against her cheek, slides his chin into the spot where her jawline curves into her neck. Alfred Hitchcock directed Grant and Bergman to nuzzle each other like that in order to circumvent the Production Code's ban on kisses longer than three seconds, but I had other reasons for remembering that particular scene.

"Pull over here," my new friend said, her eyes glistening, her lips parted seductively; she was definitely ready for her close-up, Mr. DeMille. In that moment she reminded me of a young Bette Davis, gazing up at Paul Henreid aboard the cruise ship in *Now, Voyager*. I felt a strange urge to recreate that scene from the film, the one in which Henreid lights two cigarettes in his mouth and then passes one to Bette Davis. I had no cigarettes, though; I didn't smoke, and I never had.

I parked the car on the plateau above the river, and with no code limiting our actions, she guided my hands gently around her own curves as she made softer, slower, earthier sounds, expressing a different kind of elation. Then we climbed down the cliffside to the river and skinny-dipped in the cold water, and when she burst up through the water's swirling, foaming skin with her black hair plastered to her chest and shoulders, like Ava Gardner in *Pandora and the Flying Dutchman*, my heart rate accelerated to the point that I thought I would either pass out or explode.

I had never felt anything like the way I felt that night. It was like stepping from a black-and-white B movie into a colour-saturated 3D computer-animated epic. My senses were nearly overloaded, and yet I was ready for more.

In the film *Don Juan*, John Barrymore set a record for the number of kisses given in a single film (he planted his lips on his two leading ladies, Estelle Taylor and Mary Astor, a total of 127 times during the movie's two-hour run time); the longest onscreen kiss in film history was between Jane Wyman and Regis Toomey (of all actors) in the comedy *You're in the Army Now* (of all films); and I resolved to break both Toomey's and Barrymore's records with my new friends. Practically every soft-focused, dramatically lit romantic scene from every 1940s movie I had ever watched replayed itself on my mind's screen, and I recast myself as the leading man in all of them.

With the right leading lady, I would recreate Humphrey Bogart's sexy, face-holding kiss upon the lips of Mary Astor in *The Maltese Falcon*, and the kiss I would receive in return would be long and slow, like the candlelight-backlit kiss between Vivien Leigh and Robert Taylor in *Waterloo Bridge*, with the flashing lights and flickering neon of Clifton Hill standing in for the candles.

Yes, the 1940s had been a great decade for romance in Hollywood, but the 1990s were off to a great start for me personally, and I had to wonder if perhaps my sisters were a bit jealous. While they continued to spend their lives onstage, following the directions of scripted adventures, mouthing the words of meticulously plotted dramas, laughing on cue at predetermined delights, and simulating having fun, I was doing it all for real.

I had escaped.

And, eventually, for the first time in our seventeen years together, my sisters would follow my lead.

Scene 21:

The Extracurriculars

(Or: Sunrise)

EACH IN THEIR OWN way, my sisters began initiating their own escape plans.

One day at lunchtime, as I was about to sneak away from school to meet one of my new friends for an afternoon rendezvous, Violet spotted me in the hallway through the open cafeteria doors.

She was sitting with three other girls, all sporting spiked, dyed-neon-pink hair, all clad entirely in black; Violet had recently taken to emulating this style herself, stopping in the girls' washroom after school each day to change her clothes and wash the pink spray dye out of her hair before heading to rehearsal at the Orpheum-Galaxie.

"Errol!" she shouted. "Hey, wait up!"

Violet sprinted from the cafeteria and cornered me against the speckle-painted cinderblock wall. Her three dining companions appeared behind her.

Violet demanded, "How the hell are you getting away with this, Errol?"

"Yeah," one of the other girls reiterated.

Violet lowered her voice. "None of us are going to rat on you, okay? We just want to know how you're doing it, that's all."

One of the other girls grumbled, "We skip out once in a while to have a band practice, and every time we get slapped with detention."

The second girl continued the complaint. "Meanwhile, you saunter out of here every other day, whenever you feel like it —"

"And none of us have ever seen you in detention," the third black-clad girl concluded.

Of the three, I recognized this one: her previously dyed-black hair was now spiked and dyed pink, but she wore almost the same uniform as on the day I'd met her on the first day of grade nine: silver skull earrings, black jeans, black vinyl riding boots, and her now-trademark black T-shirt with the words "ANARCHY NOW" printed upon it in white Gothic letters. I recalled that her name was Matilda.

I looked at Violet. "You're in a band?"

She ran her fingers through her spiky, temporarily pink hair. "Yeah. We got together in music class. We've had a few jam sessions." She lowered her voice to a whisper, speaking just to me. "Don't tell our father, okay?"

I had to know more. "What's the name of your band?"

Violet glanced around at her bandmates and proclaimed, "We're calling ourselves … Kitty Galore."

"KITTY POWER!" Matilda hollered, raising her fist in the air.

"KITTY POWER!" the others screamed in response, mimicking the fist-pumping gesture.

Matilda explained, "It's a play on Pussy Galore from that James Bond movie."

"Gold-fingaaaaaaaah!" sang one of the as-yet-unidentified bandmates. "We wanted to call ourselves Pussy Power, but there's no way that the principal will let us play in the talent show with that name."

"So ... what sort of music do you ladies play? Cocktail jazz? Or ... I know. You're a baroque string quartet."

They all rolled their eyes at me. I rolled my eyes back at them; admittedly, I hadn't bothered learning much about current pop culture, but it was obvious, even to me, that they were a punk band.

Violet gestured at her bandmates. "Tiger Kitty plays guitar, Cheetah Kitty plays the drums, and Matilda — Leopard Kitty — plays bass."

Tiger Kitty slapped Violet on the shoulder and bellowed, "And this girl's voice ROCKS OUR WORLD!" with Cheetah Kitty adding helpfully, "Cougar Kitty screams 'em like she creams 'em."

"Well, that's terrific," I said, ducking around the members of Kitty Galore. "I can't wait for your first concert."

"Hey, wait a minute," Violet said as the members of Kitty Galore surrounded me again in the middle of the hall. "How are you skipping so much school without getting caught?"

Without any other option, I reluctantly pulled the note from my pocket and showed it to Violet.

To Whom it May Concern,

Please excuse my grandson, Errol Trouper, from his classes at Fallsview District High School this afternoon. He has an appointment.

Sincerely,

Chrysanthemum Trouper

"Get outta here," Violet gasped. "Making our poor little granny complicit in your crimes? Shame on you, Errol Trouper."

"It's not exactly a lie," I said. "I do have an appointment … with Yvonne."

"Hey, I'm not criticizing. Getting Grandma to write you a note for a booty call … you're my friggin' hero."

And with those rare words of admiration spoken, she snatched the note from my hand. "Girls! Girls!" she cried, sprinting away from me. "Gimme a pen."

One of them did, and, scribbling quickly with the page pressed against a cinderblock wall, Violet added this:

PS — Please also excuse my granddaughter Violet Trouper (aka Cougar Kitty) today and on any other day that she needs to practice with her band Kitty Galore. This also applies to her bandmates, Tiger, Cheetah, and Leopard Kitty.

Violet handed the modified page back to me and said, "There. Go give that to the principal."

"Seriously?

"Seriously."

When I handed the note to him, he read it, sighed, and simply said, "See you tomorrow," before thinking to add, "And by the way, if you would be so kind as to inform your grandmother that the school's marching band quite desperately needs a new tuba and a few new trombones …"

"See?" Violet said when I emerged from the office with the news. "Money can most definitely buy love. Wanna give us a ride to our rehearsal, bro?"

"Umm … the Floride won't fit five people. And I'm already late to meet up with Yvonne."

Violet shrugged. "It's only a ten-minute drive. Matilda — Leopard Kitty — can sit on my lap, and you can pop the trunk open and Tiger and Cheetah can ride in the back. You'll just have to drive slow."

Cheetah Kitty, who was lean and muscular from kicking and pummelling the hell out of her drums on a daily basis, purred, "Or maybe I'll sit on your brother's lap instead. And we can drive fast. So it's nice and bumpy." She reached over and slapped me on the ass.

"Okay," I acquiesced. "I'll give you ladies a ride to your rehearsal."

OLIVIA'S ESCAPE PLAN MAY have seemed less outwardly rebellious than Violet's, but it was more meticulously crafted, and therefore it was the most likely to actually succeed.

Olivia was by far the most successful student of the Trouper Quintuplets; she had earned top grades in every one of her classes at FDHS, and she planned on applying for early admission to the business schools at several prominent universities.

She approached me late one evening, when she was sure that everyone else at Trouper Terrace was asleep (although I knew that Violet had snuck out to go see a band called Bikini Kill at a club in Buffalo with the other members of Kitty Galore, Marigold was up in the tower reading an Anaïs Nin novel she'd smuggled home from the library, our father was out for the evening, cavorting with one or more of his co-stars for all I knew, and Grandma Trouper was still awake in her upstairs chambers, drinking bourbon and smoking Cuban cigars on her balcony).

"Errol," Olivia ventured, "do you think you could drive me to some interviews?"

"Interviews?"

"Yes. For early admission scholarships." She hesitated. "Just in case our father talks Grandma out of signing the cheques when I want to leave for university. I don't want to be stuck traipsing across the stage at the Orpheum-Galaxie for the rest of my life."

I understood completely. "Sure, I'll drive. Just give me the dates, and I'll book off the time."

Behind her business-as-usual expression, behind the reflective lenses of her glasses, there was a hopeful glimmer in Olivia's eyes that I rarely ever saw.

Then she handed me three neatly typed letters.

"I took the liberty of drafting these for you. All they need is Grandma Trouper's signature."

Then she shook my hand and turned and walked away.

MARIGOLD'S PLAN FOR HER next act of defiance was both ambitious and complex.

One evening, while we were working together to assemble yet another jigsaw puzzle atop the stage in the basement of Trouper Terrace (which we still did whenever one of us was experiencing insomnia), Marigold snapped a series of pieces together in rapid succession, as if suddenly possessed. Then, in a trance-like way, she said calmly, "I'm going to rescue Mom."

"You're going to ...?"

"I'm going to rescue Mom. And you're going to help me."

She suggested a preliminary reconnaissance mission to the Sunrise Mental Health and Addiction Recovery Colony to visit our mother, to see if she was ready to come home to Trouper

Terrace again, and, if so, to collude with her to orchestrate plans for her assisted escape.

"Are you with me, Errol? I'll need a driver."

I had already said yes to Olivia and Violet (and the rest of the members of Kitty Galore), so how could I say no to Marigold? Especially when her mission was so selfless, so bold.

"I'm with you, Marigold."

"I knew you would be," she said, and she reached over the half-completed puzzle to hug me. She was the only one of my sisters who ever did that.

We would leave the next day. I wouldn't need to coax Grandma Trouper into signing yet another Get Out of School Free card for me and Marigold, since by that time the office staff at Fallsview District High School didn't bother issuing truant slips to any of the Fabulous Trouper Quintuplets. Besides, I wasn't sure that I wanted our father's mother to know about our secret mission to the Sunrise Colony; it was, after all, Chrysanthemum Trouper's signature on the cheques that paid for our mother's continued incarceration there.

Marigold agreed with my assessment of the situation. "It's probably best not to tell Grandma Trouper. And definitely don't tell our father. In fact, maybe we shouldn't tell anyone."

So, without a word to any other Trouper, Marigold packed her angel-winged backpack with snacks and beverages for the ride, and we left at sunrise, arriving at our destination later that morning.

The hillside into which the boxy, postmodern-style institution was built obscured the impending sunset, but since the building faced east, those windows likely allowed for a pretty decent view of the sunrise each morning; in that respect, the Sunrise Mental

Health and Addiction Recovery Colony seemed to deliver at least part of what its name promised.

"It's not exactly Green Manors, is it?" Marigold quipped, referring to the rather lavish mental asylum in which Ingrid Bergman played a psychiatric doctor in Alfred Hitchcock's *Spellbound*.

As we entered the cool, unadorned, fluorescent-lit foyer of the institution, the shrivelled, bespectacled nurse at the front desk eyed us with suspicion. I whispered to Marigold, "And she's not exactly Ingrid Bergman, either."

Marigold informed the nurse, "We're here to see Lily Royale-Trouper."

"Really?" the nurse said. "She hasn't had a visitor in over three years."

Marigold and I glanced incredulously at each other; our father hadn't visited our mother once in all this time?

"We're her children," Marigold assured the nurse with that sweet, sincere voice of hers. "My brother just got his driver's licence. We had no way to get here until now."

"Okay, then," the nurse sighed. "Follow me."

"Lily," the nurse said, "you've got visitors." Then she left us to face our mother for the first time in a very, very long time.

As soon as we walked through the door and into that sparsely furnished, antiseptic-smelling room, Marigold and I both knew that we were never, ever going to meet that Ingrid-Bergman-meets-Grace-Kelly-meets-Barbara-Stanwyck-meets-Ava-Gardner version of our mother. She looked as if she had aged thirty years since the day of her uncredited cameo appearance in our father's production of *Cyrano de Bergerac*. She had withered away to a mere husk of her former self, which is probably what happens when someone who subsists almost entirely on alcohol has it suddenly and completely removed from them.

"Hi, Mom," Marigold said.

I echoed, "Hi, Mom."

She didn't say anything for a long time.

Finally, our mother broke the ear-ringing silence by saying, "Are you still reading a book a day, Mari-Girl?"

"Well, it's a book every few days now, Mom. But they're longer ones."

"I saw you looking at the book on my nightstand. That's what reminded me. That's why I asked."

She reached for the hardcover volume atop the bare table beside her bleached-white hospital cot, but her fingers stopped halfway.

"It's a biography of Grace Kelly. Her acting career ended after she agreed to marry Prince Rainier III of Monaco."

She reached for the book again, but once more her hand stopped halfway.

"She got to call herself a princess, but she lost herself at the same time."

She turned to gaze out through the small window behind the faux-woodgrain-veneered headboard of her cot, but it was dark outside by then, and there was nothing to see.

"My mother had the same car as Princess Grace. Except it was a convertible, not a coupe. I drove it for a while, too. Do you remember?"

Both Marigold and I nodded, but neither of us said anything; there was no point in mentioning that the same car was parked outside, wearing the scrapes and dents from our mother's final joyride.

"It wasn't the car that Princess Grace died in, though," our mother said, her attention moving from the window to the book again.

She reached out once more, and this time her frail fingers snatched the Grace Kelly biography from the night table. She offered it to Marigold.

"You should read this," she said. "We could talk about it the next time you come to visit me."

Marigold held the book against her chest. "Sure, Mom," she said. "I'll read it."

I knew that she would.

Then the tears finally burst from our mother's glassy eyes.

"Please get me out of here. Please, children, please."

She aimed her sunken eyes back and forth, alternating between Marigold and me.

To Marigold: "You will be adults soon."

To me: "You'll be turning eighteen."

To Marigold: "Any immediate adult relative can sign me out of here."

To me: "Any immediate adult relative. I've read the papers."

To Marigold: "It doesn't have to be your father."

To me: "It doesn't have to be your grandmother. It can be one of you."

To Marigold: "You'll be turning eighteen soon."

To me: "Please."

To Marigold: "Please get me out of here."

Marigold promised her that we would.

I knew that it was a promise we would never be able to keep, but I didn't say so.

Eventually, the woman who was once Lily Royale fell asleep in her rocking chair, and Marigold and I walked out to the Renault Floride that had once been her mother's, that had once briefly been hers.

I started the car, and the headlights illuminated the brass-trimmed letters on the building's façade: The Sunrise Mental Health and Addiction Recovery Colony.

"Her room faces the hill," Marigold observed. "She never gets to see the sunrise."

Then she tucked the biography of Grace Kelly into her angel-winged backpack and said, "Let's go."

Scene 22:

The Replacements

(Or: One Star out of Five)

JOAN NEVER ASKED ME for a ride anywhere, nor did she ever request that Grandma Trouper sign any Get Out of School Free cards for her so she could pursue extracurricular interests; all Joan ever wanted in life was to be an actress, so she was perfectly happy to remain onstage with our father and to remain his favourite child.

Inside the Trouper-Royale Orpheum-Galaxie theatre, the final performance of the Trouper Young Star Theatre Development Program's fourth all-female production, *Top Girls*, had just wrapped, and most of the audience of beaming parents, grandparents, and siblings had already left the auditorium.

As the student actors and crew worked onstage to strike the set, their illustrious director strode out to centre stage, pausing to adjust his golden cravat. "Once again, well done, ladies," his baritone voice boomed. "This was a fine show indeed. And now it's time to take a well-earned rest, and then mark your calendars for the second week of September, when we will begin holding auditions for our next ..." (he paused for effect) "... all ... female ... show!"

I was still lingering in the auditorium, having dutifully showed up to watch my sisters in their final performance of the show, as well as our father's Nubile Minions (as my sisters and I had taken to calling John Lionel Trouper's legion of adoring, doe-eyed extras).

"I am proud to announce," the great director continued, "that the play for which I've acquired the rights for our troupe to perform next season is ..." (another dramatic pause) "*Nunsense*!"

Joan and the Nubile Minions all applauded earnestly, but Violet, Olivia, and Marigold looked distinctly less enthused, with Violet expressing their collective thoughts succinctly as usual. "*Nunsense*?" she grumbled. "Is he fucking kidding?"

"Watch your language, please, Violet," our father admonished; then, more to the Nubile Minions than to any of his offspring, he continued in dulcet tones, "And yes, *Nunsense*. It's a very popular show. We will pack the theatre for weeks."

But Violet wasn't willing to let it go. "Popularity is a warning sign. And I, for one, am not performing in any ridiculous musical comedy. Especially one about nuns."

I recognized all too well the crimson tone washing over our father's face, and Olivia did, too, wisely stepping between John Lionel and Violet.

"I think what Violet is trying to say is," Olivia said evenly, "well ... do you think maybe we're at the point where we've got the talent and experience to try something a bit more ... challenging? Like, say, *The Women*? We all love that movie, and all of us would like to give the play a try."

Our father just shrugged. "I've already bought and paid for the rights to *Nunsense* for next season."

"Then I'm out for next season," Violet announced. "There is no way in hell that I'm doing *Nunsense*."

Our father's jowls flushed red, but as he was also hyper-aware of the blinking eyes of his Nubile Minions gazing upon him, he managed to contain his outrage. "Well, Violet, you don't get to just waltz back in here and expect to be given a role when you change your mind."

"That's okay," Violet said with a crooked smirk, "I've got other things to keep me busy."

From the back corner of the auditorium, the members of Kitty Galore raised their fists in the air as a show of solidarity with Violet.

Our father's own clenched fists were trembling, but he still managed to moderate his speaking voice. "Fine, then. You're out." Then he aimed his glare around the stage, with barely contained rage burning in his eyes. "Anyone else feel like sitting this one out?"

Olivia avoided his eyes as she muttered, "Well, actually ... I'm in the running for the school's Academic Medal, and ... well, I'd maybe like to devote a bit more time to my schoolwork."

"Anyone else?" our father demanded incredulously.

Marigold looked down at her toes and said, "I think I'm ready for a break, too."

Then, to his favourite daughter, our father said, "And you, Joan?"

Joan turned to face her father as if bravely facing the sunset over her fire-scorched plantation, and she proclaimed in a quavering voice, "Never! I'll never abandon you or this stage, Daddy! I'm in this for life! I ... am an actress!"

Our father forced a smile. "You're a good girl, Joan."

Then he turned to glare at each of his other children in turn.

"As for the rest of you ungrateful ..." He straightened. "Actually, you know what? It's fine, it's fine."

He smiled and looked around at his collection of eager Nubile Minions. "Your absence will provide opportunities for other stars to shine."

And so it came to pass that, while I snuck out to have adventures with my new friends, while Violet screamed and thrashed under cover with Kitty Galore, while Olivia secretly applied for scholarships and early admissions to universities, and while Marigold covertly planned to free our mother from the Sunrise Mental Health and Addiction Recovery Colony, Joan dutifully committed all of her talent and energy to her performance as Mother Superior Mary Regina in our father's production of *Nunsense*. Of the five Fabulous Trouper Quintuplets, she was the firstborn, our father's perpetual favourite, the natural talent, the *Femme Fatale*, the Princess, the Damsel, our family's one true Drama Queen. She was the one star out of five.

And so, when Joan, along with our father's carefully selected replacement cast, hit the stage on the opening night of *Nunsense*, the rest of us Trouper Quintuplets, accompanied by the members of Kitty Galore, merely watched from the audience. And the show that we witnessed was ... well, it was truly memorable.

FOR VIOLET, OLIVIA, MARIGOLD, and I, it was truly painful to watch Joan trying her best to stay in character and deliver her usual nuanced and professional performance while our father's legion of Nubile Minions warbled and stumbled through a song-and-dance routine during the endless first act of *Nunsense*, but the members of Kitty Galore found it hilarious; their unrestrained giggles were probably at least partly caused by the effects of the fat joint they had shared outside the theatre before the show, but their conniptions of laughter were definitely amplified by the comedy of errors unfolding onstage.

"Dayyyy-ummm!" a tittering Tiger Kitty yelped. "This is awful. Can we pleeease leave during the intermission?"

Leopard Kitty (aka Matilda), who was also giggling uncontrollably from the combined effects of the weed and the onstage catastrophe in progress, added, "Yeah, come on, Cougar, let's get outta here. This is brutal."

Violet just shrugged and smiled her crooked, punk rock smirk. "Hey, we're a team, right? If I have to suffer, then the rest of you have to suffer, too."

A blurry-eyed Cheetah Kitty snorted, "Sadistic bitch!"

Stifling laughter, Violet responded, "I am the Marquis de friggin' Sade!"

Onstage, one of the Nubile Minions stopped in the middle of the dance routine to put her hands on her hips and glare at the giggling members of Kitty Galore, whom she recognized from school. This caused several other Nubile Minions to crash into her, causing them all to tumble onto the stage like high-heel-wearing dominoes.

Violet turned to Olivia in the seat beside her. "You're sober — is this really as bad as I think it is?"

Olivia cradled her face in her hands. "At least you can laugh."

"So glad I sat this one out," Violet giggled. "What a train wreck."

Olivia just sighed. "Train wrecks happen when there's no one actually driving the train. Joan says he's been more concerned with the cast liking him than with actually directing them."

"It must piss her off that he's paying more attention to them than to her."

"Oh, girl," Cheetah Kitty sniggered, "apparently your dad has been paying special attention to certain cast members. You probably don't wanna know about the rumours going around school."

Olivia's eyebrows rose to High Alert Status. "Rumours?"

"Well," Cheetah said, "you know the girl who's playing Sister Mary Hubert?"

"We call her Neon-Pink Madonna," Tiger Kitty added helpfully.

"Well," Cheetah continued, "how do I put this delicately ... the rumour is that she ... that she did some favours for your father in exchange for her role ... if you know what I mean."

"Jeezus, Cheetah!" Violet yelped. "That's putting it delicately?"

Olivia shook her head. "You girls should know better than to believe ...," but her voice trailed off as, onstage, Neon-Pink Madonna, as Sister Mary Hubert, warbled so out of key and off time that it almost seemed intentional, like Jean Hagen's performance in *Singin' in the Rain*.

"Right," Violet sighed. "It was definitely her talent that got that chick onstage."

But Olivia held firm in her disbelief. "Look, I know he's not perfect. But his previous affairs were with women, not —"

"Hey, Neon-Pink Madonna is officially a woman," Matilda contributed coolly. "She's eighteen, and she can do whatever she wants."

To which a giggling Cheetah Kitty added, "Or whoever."

As another chorus-line collision occurred onstage, the members of Kitty Galore once again erupted in conniptions of laughter, and Olivia re-buried her face in her hands.

Scene 23:

The Reviews

(Or: Scotch-Scented Santa Scrooge versus Neon-Pink Madonna's Daddy)

UNFORTUNATELY FOR OUR FATHER, the reviewers saw the same show that we did.

REVIEW

John Lionel Trouper's *Nunsense* Makes No Sense at All

*** (one out of five stars)**

By Dane Grady
Applause Magazine
November 29, 1994

Nunsense is such a fun, crowd-pleasing play that any production of it should automatically be a winner, but John Lionel Trouper's current version is an unmitigated disaster. This show is a clunky, amateurish mess, completely unworthy of its popular script, its heralded director, and the legendary theatre in which it is performed.

How has this production failed us? Oh, let me count the ways: It is woefully miscast. The singing is depressingly flat (when it isn't gratingly sharp). The dancing is unimaginatively choreographed and awkwardly executed. The story limps forward at a glacially slow pace. And, worst of all for a musical comedy, it is dreadfully unfunny (except for the parts that are supposed to be touching, which are so maudlin and overwrought that they become unintentionally hilarious).

Even the costuming is disastrous. Who decided that the characters should all strut around onstage in dangerously high heels? One dancing nun performed a particularly spectacular pratfall onstage, but I wasn't sure whether to blame her lack of dance skills, the choreography (which looked like an apocalyptic traffic jam in slow motion), or simply her ridiculous footwear.

One over-the-top high-heel-wearing nun might be amusing, but a whole convent full of sexy nuns is just silly — not to mention dangerous — and a director of John Lionel Trouper's calibre should understand the difference.

This is the fourth production of the (until now) much heralded Trouper Young Star Theatre Development Program, which affords young, often first-time actors the opportunity to hone their craft on the stage of the stalwart Trouper-Royale Orpheum-Galaxie Theatre. Because the *raison d'être* of the Young Star Program is to provide onstage experience to amateur, previously untrained cast members, there is the temptation to forgive a certain degree of ineptitude from the performers; as such, the blame for this pathetic production of *Nunsense* must fall squarely on the shoulders of its director.

In two previous seasons, John Lionel Trouper has won the coveted Best Director Award from the Western Ontario League of Dramatists for Young Star Productions, which begs the question: What went wrong this time? There is one obvious difference: in *Toad of Toad Hall* and *Steel Magnolias*, the principal roles were played by John Lionel Trouper's own daughters, Joan, Violet, Olivia, and Marigold Trouper, all seasoned performers who have been acting professionally practically since birth.

In this production, however, only Joan Trouper is in the cast, and as Mother Superior Mary Regina, she is the lone shining light in this abysmal production. Alas, her efforts are in vain, as everything else crumbles around her, burying her competent performance beneath the rubble. Nevertheless, Joan Trouper's valiant efforts earn this play one star, rather than none.

So why were the rest of the Trouper siblings excluded from this show? Perhaps this gesture was meant to be a noble one? Perhaps the director meant to give meatier roles to the amateurs in this production? Whatever the reason, without a core cast of professionals to support the beginners and help keep their heads above water, this production of *Nunsense* sinks faster than the RMS *Titanic*.

> A note to John Lionel Trouper: Get your kids back onstage. And maybe hand those Best Director trophies over to them while you're at it.

And this review was the most charitable one. Others utilized practically every synonym for "terrible" in existence: "dreadful," "awful," "appalling," "horrendous," "atrocious," "abominable," "deplorable," "egregious," "abhorrent," "ghastly," "grim," "dire," "sickening," "vile," and even "vomitous."

DURING THE WEEKS THAT followed, we saw even less of our father than usual. He sequestered himself inside his office in the basement of Trouper Terrace, emerging only to deposit empty liquor bottles in the garbage can and to stagger upstairs to his bedroom at the end of each day.

His double-breasted navy blue suit, his ivory French-cuffed shirt, and his golden silk cravat lay on the floor in his room where he had discarded them after the final show of *Nunsense*, and he shuffled around Trouper Terrace late at night — and eventually during the daytime as well — in a blouse-like nightgown and an old-fashioned sleeping cap, trading in his Hitchcock-meets-Gable-meets-Spielberg look for a costume resembling Alastair Sim as Ebenezer Scrooge in the 1951 version of *A Christmas Carol*.

When he had emptied his last jar of Doctor MacRumplehyde's Eternal Youth Pomade (the special-order black-tinted grease that he used to slick back and conceal his thinning, greying hair), he didn't bother making a trip to the drugstore to order more, and his hair soon became a wild, matted rat's nest. When he abandoned his twice-daily habit of shaving, the lower half of his face was soon obscured by a shaggy, mostly white beard. In a matter of weeks, his look transformed from that of a high-mileage but well-maintained Hollywood icon to an alcoholic shopping mall Santa who had fallen off the sleigh.

John Lionel's normally shatterproof ego had finally been cracked by the consistent pummelling from all directions of his first musical, and it added insult to injury (and some additional *real* injuries as well) when the fuming, coverall-clad, handlebar-moustachioed father of Neon-Pink Madonna came pounding on the door of Trouper Terrace.

"You're gonna pay for what you did to my daughter!" Neon-Pink Madonna's Daddy raged as he forced his way into the foyer, raising his fists in our father's face.

"Who is your daughter?"

"She played the lead role in your most recent play."

"Oh, that one," our father moaned. "The biggest casting mistake I ever made."

"Having your way with her was the biggest mistake you ever made!" Neon-Pink Madonna's Daddy hollered, charging our father.

"Having my ... no, no, no. It was all I could do to keep her away from me!"

Then the Scotch-Scented Santa Scrooge absorbed several punches from Neon-Pink Madonna's Daddy, and due to his nutrient-deprived, alcohol-impaired state, the (formerly) Great John Lionel Trouper crashed dramatically onto the floor before struggling back to his feet to utter another slurred proclamation of innocence. This scene repeated itself several times before our grandmother was able to step between her precious only son and the outraged pugilist.

"Step aside, grandma," Neon-Pink Madonna's Daddy huffed.

"When I'm finished with him, this old pervert ain't gonna mess around with any teenage girls any time soon."

"'Old perv ...,'" Chrysanthemum Trouper sputtered, moving closer to block the intruder from going at her son again. "Why, how dare you, sir! My John Lionel would never. He would never! He has daughters of his own! He would never!"

"Fine, then," he said, turning away. "I ain't gonna hit no old lady. If you won't get outta the way and let him take his medicine like a man, then I'm just gonna go to the cops. He'll get it a lot worse once he's behind bars."

"Well, it's your word against ours," our grandmother hissed. "I hope that you can afford a brilliant lawyer, because *we* can."

Neon-Pink Madonna's Daddy lowered his voice. "Well, now, your son has a bit of a reputation around town, don't he? Shouldn't be too difficult to collect some corroborating evidence to support our claim."

Chrysanthemum Trouper quickly regained her legendary composure. "Now, now, sir, wait just a moment," she said in a flat, businesslike tone. "I'm sure that we can resolve this misunderstanding in a more civilized fashion."

Neon-Pink Madonna's Daddy lowered his fists and raised his chin. "And what exactly are you offering?"

As the executive director and chief financial officer for all of our father's theatrical endeavours, Chrysanthemum Trouper was on the hook for all of the production expenses for *Nunsense*, official and unofficial, so she cleverly disguised this particular expense by writing "The First Annual Trouper Young Star Theatre Scholarship Award" on the memo line beside her signature. Neon-Pink Madonna's Daddy's eyes bulged when he saw the amount written on the cheque.

"Please, do convey my personal congratulations to your

talented daughter for being chosen to receive this very lucrative prize," our grandmother said sweetly. "Just one final thing — shall I make this out to you, or to her?"

"To me, I guess."

"You will hold the funds in trust for her, then, I'm sure," said our grandmother, with only the slightest hint of condescension in her voice.

Neon-Pink Madonna's Daddy looked around our grandmother to cast a long, dark stare at the Scotch-Scented Santa Scrooge, then he turned and walked out of Trouper Terrace, his swollen knuckles clenched tightly around the cheque.

Our father crumpled onto the floor again, without any punching or pushing this time. He stayed there for a long time, curled up in the fetal position, before finally crawling to the stairs and up to his room, muttering, "I didn't do anything wrong. I didn't do anything wrong."

It would have been an award-winning performance if it hadn't been for real.

Scene 24:

The Producer

(Or: Like Queen Victoria Possessed by Josephine Baker)

DURING THE MONTHS THAT followed, our grandmother's bourbon intake tripled, and she seemed to forgo sleeping altogether. The furrows in her brow deepened, and her blue eyes lost their twinkle and sank deeper into their sockets. For the first time in her eighty years, Chrysanthemum Trouper looked her actual age, perhaps because for the first time in her sixty-two years as John Lionel's mother, she had been unable to buy a happy ending for her precious only son.

But then one morning she woke up with an idea: she would provide her John Lionel — and maybe the rest of us, too — with a happy beginning instead.

It was before dawn when Chrysanthemum Trouper emerged from her chambers dressed in her finest ensemble, her barrel-shaped torso cloaked in her favourite royal purple satin dress, with its puffed velvet sleeves and French lace collar. Her neck was encircled with three chunky chains of gold and jewels (ancient engagement gifts from her former industrialist husband), and her head was crowned with a headdress of peacock feathers (a souvenir from her Ziegfeld Follies days). Upon another octogenarian woman, this outfit would have seemed comical, and maybe even a little deranged, but our grandmother carried it off with her head held high, like Queen Victoria possessed by Josephine Baker.

She stood outside our bedrooms in the upstairs hallway, clanging a big, loud hand bell (a prop from some play, I suppose).

"Wake up, my loves! Wake up."

We all emerged through our doorways, rumpled and squint-eyed, as our grandmother announced, "We will meet together this morning at the Orpheum-Galaxie Theatre in exactly one hour."

"But, Grandma," a sleepy Olivia protested, "we've got school."

"This is more important, my dear." The sparkle had returned to her eyes. "Don't worry, though, I'll write a note to your principal to excuse your absence."

Our grandmother then turned toward her precious and only son, who had been the last one to stumble into the hallway. "John Lionel, you will take a bath, shave off that hideous beard, and fix your hair in a manner befitting a gentleman of your stature." From the fingers that weren't holding the bell, she handed her bedraggled son a fresh jar of Doctor MacRumplehyde's Eternal Youth Pomade. "And then you will iron your suit, and you will wear it. Your role as a stinking, self-pitying house tramp will come to an end this morning."

Our father looked down at his untrimmed toenails, refusing to meet her gaze.

"I will stand it no more, John Lionel!" she bellowed. "From this moment forward, you will dress, speak, and act like the refined gentleman that I raised you to be!"

"Yes, Mother," our father muttered. He took the jar of pomade and shuffled back into his room, closing the door behind him.

Then our grandmother turned toward Joan, Violet, Olivia, Marigold, and me.

"Children, go put on your best clothes. Violet, that means no spikes or pink paint in your hair, and absolutely no ripped jeans. You will borrow a dress from Joan."

"Okay, Gram," Violet said.

Joan's mouth gaped open in protest, but our grandmother raised a hand and said coolly, "Joan, you will lend your sister one of your dresses. A nice one."

Joan drew in a breath and said, "Yes, Grandmother."

"And Marigold, dear, please leave the backpack with the angel wings at home. You are a young woman now, not a little girl."

"Yes, Grandma."

"Olivia, you will bring along a pen and notepad, and you will transcribe everything that is discussed this morning so that there will be no misunderstandings later. Understood?"

"Yes, Grandma Trouper."

"And Errol, you will need to be ready in half an hour so you can drive me to the theatre. The rest of you fit young things can walk; the exercise will do your constitutions some good."

I nodded. "I'll be ready in fifteen minutes."

"Good boy," said our bejewelled, satin-and-velvet-wrapped grandmother, smiling regally from beneath her towering headdress. So, like the von Trapp children in *The Sound of Music*, we all did about-face manoeuvres and marched into our rooms to get ready. In exactly one hour, scrubbed, polished, and dressed in our finest, we would all be gathered onstage at the Orpheum-Galaxie.

POSITIONED AT CENTRE STAGE was a long, narrow table, which had served as a prop in several Trouper theatre productions, ranging from *The NEW Scallywags* to *Cyrano de Bergerac* to the ill-fated *Nunsense*. Initially, I had placed the chairs on both sides of the table, facing each other, but our grandmother insisted on a different arrangement.

"No! No! No, Errol!" she scolded. "We are setting the stage for a great monologue. This is not to be a table reading, and it will certainly not be a discussion or a debate. This is to be a performance; perhaps the second most important of my career."

So, I rearranged the chairs so they all faced the empty auditorium, and our grandmother seated herself at the exact midpoint of the table, her face glowing with a beatific, halo-like patina, courtesy of the spotlight she'd had me aim at her from the balcony. Then, one by one, the rest of the Trouper family joined her, taking their seats and turning to face Chrysanthemum like the Apostles in Leonardo da Vinci's painting *The Last Supper*; although there were only half the number of Troupers at this table as Apostles in da Vinci's painting, Olivia, Marigold, Violet, Joan, and I, and especially our father, tried to make up for it by appearing twice as attentive and expressive as our holy counterparts.

Chrysanthemum Trouper then raised her chin, placed her hands palms-up on the tabletop like the genie in a fortune-telling machine, and drew a deep breath. "My brilliant and accomplished son and my precious, gifted grandchildren," she regally intoned, "I have served as this family's executive producer for more years than you children have been alive, without expectation of thanks, reward, or recompense. I have provided the funds for more productions than I can count, for as long as the Trouper family name has graced the marquee of this celebrated playhouse."

Marigold leaned over and whispered to me and Olivia, with a note of defiance in her voice, "Should I remind her that our mother's family name also 'graces the marquee' of this celebrated playhouse? And that she also 'provides the funds for' our mother's continued imprisonment?"

Olivia admonished in a hissing whisper, "Shush, Marigold!"

Our grandmother cast a quick, icy glare at Marigold and Olivia, halting any further whispers, then she continued boldly, "So, my loves, as the chief financial officer of our family, it pains me to announce that we Troupers find ourselves in a dire financial predicament, from which we will extract ourselves only with the participation of each and every one of us. No one gets to opt out this time. If we are to save this family and restore our good name, it will take all of our talents and efforts combined."

She then slapped both hands down on the tabletop and stood up as straight as her ailing back would allow, imitating the bravado of a wartime speech by Sir Winston Churchill, right down to the quavering voice and the shaking jowls.

"So, who is with me?" she cried. "Who will help save our home, our theatre, our family name? Who is with me?"

Joan was the first to jump to her feet. "I'm with you, Grandmother!"

Rising just a beat behind his favourite daughter, John Lionel proclaimed, "I am also with you, Mother."

One by one, Olivia, Violet, and I also stood up; what choice did we have, really?

Conspicuously, a frowning Marigold was the last to reluctantly join the rest of us.

Scene 25:

The Casting Call

(Or: No Time to Waste)

JOAN, VIOLET, OLIVIA, MARIGOLD, and I spent a sleepless night waiting as our father and his mother sequestered themselves behind closed doors to plan and strategize for the grand rebirth of the Troupers, and in the morning, we reconvened around the long table atop the stage at the Orpheum-Galaxie Theatre. All eyes were upon our grandmother as she settled, queen-like, into her spotlight-illuminated chair.

"It pleases me greatly to announce to you all today," she pronounced, "that the next show to be performed at the Trouper-Royale Orpheum-Galaxie will be a play written in 1936 by Clare Boothe Luce. And the name of the play is ... *The Women*."

My four sisters immediately began cheering and clapping. *The Women* had been their favourite film since they were pre-pubescent girls, and it was maybe the only thing upon which they have ever all agreed. Our grandmother raised her chin and smiled with tight lips as her granddaughters regaled her with applause.

All I could do was sigh. "Well, I guess that leaves me out. Again. But good luck to the rest of you. Break a leg."

"You're wrong, Errol," our grandmother said. "You will have a very important role in this production."

"*The Women* is famous for its all-female cast, Grandma. So, by default, I'm out."

"No, Errol, you are in. You are going to be the assistant director."

"With all my respect to you, Grandma ..." (and I took a moment to cast a cold glance at our father) "... I've mopped the stage and fetched coffee for the director as many times as I'm ever going to."

Chrysanthemum took a moment of her own to cast some shade in John Lionel's direction, then she turned to me and continued, "Errol, you will never be asked to pick up a mop or fetch anything for anyone. In this production, you will perform the role of a real assistant director. Your father will be the director, but you, Errol, will take notes from him, and you — and you alone — will communicate these notes to the actresses."

John Lionel pounded his fists on the tabletop. "My success as a director comes from the personal rapport that I'm able to establish with my actors! That connection simply cannot be filtered through another person!"

Once again Chrysanthemum turned her regal gaze upon her son. "As I am sure you recall, John Lionel, that 'connection,' as you so quaintly call it, was very costly to our previous show, so I must insist on a safeguard to prevent your 'connections' from becoming an issue again."

Our father was about to protest, but our grandmother silenced him with a single raised eyebrow and said, "To further clarify: in this show, all communication between the director and the actresses will go through the assistant director. You will not speak directly with any of the young women in the cast. Furthermore, during the run of the show, Errol will also serve as the stage manager. You, John Lionel, will not be backstage at any time, and in particular, you will never be anywhere near the green room nor any of the dressing rooms."

"But, Mother, I —"

"Your funding is absolutely dependent upon these conditions being met, John Lionel. So, are you perfectly clear about these parameters? Look me in the eyes when you answer."

Our father lowered his chin, but raised his eyes to meet his mother's. "I am, Mother."

Chrysanthemum turned her gaze toward her granddaughters, and her face broke into a wide smile. "All right, John Lionel ... let's not keep them in suspense any longer."

Our father also smiled brightly at his daughters, but he avoided looking at me as he spoke.

"So, then," the great director pronounced, "here are my initial casting choices for this production. First, as Crystal Allen, the role originally played in the film version of *The Women* by Joan Crawford ..."

He paused for dramatic effect and enjoyed watching Joan squirming on the edge of her seat.

"Crystal Allen will be played by ... Joan!"

Joan leaped up from her seat, squealing, and threw her arms around our father, and then our grandmother. "Thank you, thank you, thank you, Daddy! Thank you, thank you, thank you, Grandma! I will put everything I've got into this role! I will not let you down!"

Violet grumbled under her breath, "As God is my witness, I'll never be hungry again," but the crooked, cynical smirk vanished from her face the moment that our father turned to her.

"Violet," he said grandly, "you will be cast as Mary Haines, as originally played by Norma Shearer — the role with the most lines and stage time in the whole production."

I wondered what our father could possibly have been thinking; on the list of Female Character Archetypes, Mary Haines fell squarely into the "Nurturing Mother / Martyr" category, a type completely opposite our feisty, rebellious, punk rock Violet. As the official assistant director, I could have spoken up, but as usual, Violet beat me to the punch.

"There is no way in hell that I'm playing that simpering, subservient society dame," Violet protested. "It's completely outside my zone."

In hindsight, I think I maybe understand why our father wanted to cast Violet against type as Mary Haines: in *The Women,* Mary's archenemy is the gold-digging man-eater Crystal Allen, with whom Mary's husband has an affair. Norma Shearer, who played Mary Haines in the film, and Joan Crawford, as Crystal, were fierce rivals in real life. Both women were under contract to MGM Studios, and although Crawford felt that she was the superior actress, Shearer always landed better roles, presumably because of her marriage to Irving Thalberg, MGM's production chief. Joan and Norma's animosity toward each other played out to great effect in their scenes together as Crystal and Mary in *The Women*, and perhaps our father was hoping for similar onstage fireworks from his two least compatible daughters.

Since Violet refused the role, though, our father did the predictable thing and cast "Old Reliable" Olivia as Mary Haines. Olivia accepted her part in an equally predictable manner, smiling a resigned, obligatory smile and saying, "I'll do my best," which, of course, she would. While there wouldn't be the same natural friction between Olivia and Joan, John Lionel knew that Olivia would learn her lines and deliver them without a single stumble, and that he could count on Joan to ramp up the drama herself in Crystal Allen's scenes with Mary Haines.

Our father's next idea was for Violet to play the feisty, rough-edged, tough-talking Miriam Aarons, the role performed so perfectly in the movie by Paulette Goddard ... but Violet balked at that idea, too.

"Stop typecasting me all the time!"

"Stop typecasting ...?" Our father was dumbfounded now; he was unaccustomed to having his directorial wisdom questioned so brazenly. "But ...," he stammered, "I just offered you a role that is completely, diametrically opposed to —"

"I want the Rosalind Russell part," Violet said. "Sylvia, the big-mouthed gossip!"

John Lionel glanced at Joan, then at Violet, and he stroked his chin, considering. "Actually, that could work. Crystal Allen and Sylvia Fowler have a huge blowout at the end of the story. That could be terrific!"

He rubbed his freshly shaven face some more. "In that case ... Marigold, do you want the Paulette Goddard role, then?"

To be honest, I wasn't sure how she would respond. The Marigold I had always known usually shied away from overtly sassy roles, but I wasn't sure what to expect from the new, plucky, let's-break-Mom-out-of-the-asylum version of my otherwise mild-mannered sister.

"Yeah, whatever," she said. "I'll do it."

John Lionel Trouper then scratched his head through a thick layer of Doctor MacRumplehyde's Eternal Youth Pomade. "Okay, then, now that's all settled ... who do we cast in the Mary Boland part, as the Countess? I could put in a call to —"

Our grandmother sat up and puffed out her bosom. "I will play the part."

All of the other Troupers struggled to supress their surprise and shock. Our father coughed, blinked, and then coughed again. "You ... you want to play the Countess, who profits from her failed marriages to wealthy men? Do you ... do you think you can pull it off, Mother?"

Chrysanthemum, ignoring her son's sarcasm, said loudly and clearly, "I will play the part."

"Okay ...," our father stammered, "um ... that's ... terrific! It's only been ... what? Sixty or so years since you were last onstage?"

"It's just like riding a bicycle, John Lionel. You just get right back on and ride."

Our father recognized that he was not in any position to argue with his mother on this or any other point, so he began handing out production schedules and scripts.

"For the supporting roles, I'll get on the phone to some union actors ... in the meantime, the timing is going to be tight for this show, and our schedule is going to be very busy, so we will begin right now with a table reading. Errol can read the parts of the absent characters, and —"

An alarmed Olivia spoke up. "But we have school today.

"Not to worry, my ever-worried dear," our father brayed, patting Olivia on the head in a patronizing way. "I've already called you all in sick. This is more important than school, anyway."

As everyone else opened their scripts, Olivia looked genuinely ill. She turned to me and whispered, "I'm under a lot of pressure right now, Errol. This is the biggest role I've ever had, and our family's fortunes are depending on it. But I don't want my grades to suffer, either. I'm going to need top marks if next year I'm going to ..." Her voice trailed off.

"Hey, come on, Olivia. You can handle it. You're 'Old Reliable.' You'll kill the role and get the grades."

She waved the production schedule at me. "Have you had a look at this yet?"

I took my first glance at the schedule. "Yeah, wow. That is a lot of shows. But we'll pull it off. You'll see."

Olivia shook her head. "Look at the date of the final show."

I read it from the sheet. "May 25, 1995." Then I understood. "Our birthday."

"Our eighteenth birthday," Olivia said. "We'll legally be adults. We'll be officially in charge of our own destinies. We'll be free." Her tone darkens. "And I don't know about you, Errol, but when the curtain closes on that final show, I'll be taking my final bow."

Our father's voice boomed in our direction. "Olivia! There is no time to waste here!"

Olivia opened her script and answered sweetly, "You're right, Father. There isn't."

Scene 26:

The Women

(Or: Palpable Tension)

AND, SOMEHOW, WE MADE it. We made it to the evening of May 25, 1995, the collective eighteenth birthday of the Fabulous Trouper Quintuplets and the closing night performance of our production of *The Women*. The reviews were unanimous: the Troupers' version of the show was a resounding success.

REVIEW

The Troupers' *The Women* is PERFECT!

******* (five out of five stars)**

By Dane Grady
Applause Magazine
May 8, 1995

The Troupers' stage production of *The Women* is a comedic — and dramatic — *tour de force*. The tension is so thick, you can cut it with a nail file. Director John Lionel Trouper's daughters, aka the Fabulous Trouper

> Sisters, drive an all-professional, all-female dream cast who seem intent on incinerating one another with innuendoes and double entendres in every single scene.
>
> The Trouper Sisters were born to play these roles. They deliver Clare Boothe Luce's acerbic, cynical dialogue with maximum vigour and venom, and the audience expects them to begin clawing out one another's eyeballs at any moment. This play has a level of palpable tension unseen in the film or in any stage revival since then.

If there was "palpable tension" onstage, it certainly had a lot to do with our father's final casting choices, which he made without consulting me, our grandmother, or any of my sisters.

In the role of Lucy, John Lionel cast a woman with whom he had shared the stage on many occasions … and the stage floor at least once: the notorious Prudence Petty. Fragments of our father's photographs of Prudence still appeared on the basement floor of Trouper Terrace from time to time.

If that wasn't bad enough, our father also cast Prudence's nine-year-old daughter, Penny, as Little Mary, the role played in the movie by talented child actress Virginia Weidler. Penny was a born actress: mature, expressive, well-spoken, and responsive to direction, and the fact that she bore more than a passing resemblance to John Lionel did not go unnoticed by anyone.

As if this mother-and-daughter casting choice didn't add enough fuel to the already roaring flames, our father stoked the fires even further by calling on yet another woman from his past to play Edith Phelps Potter: Amber Anderson, who had played the Duenna in *Cyrano de Bergerac*. Although he had been forced by "extenuating circumstances" to fire Amber from *Cyrano*, apparently the two had kept in touch over the years, and there were no hard feelings between them; in fact, the way that they laughed and drank and flirted with each other offstage suggested that their relationship had remained rather warm.

As past competitors for our father's affections, Prudence and Amber were definitely not pleased to see each other on the first day of rehearsals, and, for obvious reasons, my sisters were even less delighted about sharing the stage with Amber and Prudence; so, if it seemed like the actresses onstage were "intent on incinerating one another" and "clawing out one another's eyeballs," well, they really were.

The Troupers' *The Women* is PERFECT! (cont.)

This production of *The Women* tips its hat frequently to the 1939 film version, but the Trouper Sisters transform themselves into empowered New Century versions of the film's famous actresses.

Olivia Trouper, in certainly her best role to date, plays the practical, devoted mother Mary Haines with added self-assurance, as if Norma Shearer's version of the character earned a PhD and started her own business after leaving her husband.

Joan Trouper's performance of Crystal Allen is certainly reminiscent of Hollywood icon Joan Crawford, but she brings an added level of aggressive sexuality to the role that even Joan wouldn't have dared under the Production Code in 1939.

Violet Trouper earns as many laughs as Rosalind Russell did as Sylvia Fowler, but Violet plays the character with an added dimension of no-nonsense

> feminist bravado, which plays to great effect against Olivia's all-knowing Mary Haines and Joan's manipulative, man-eating Crystal Allen.
>
> When Marigold Trouper's Miriam Aarons shows up halfway into the proceedings, she ups the ante on Paulette Goddard's brash, self-confident portrayal of the social-climbing showgirl, which creates a recipe for spontaneous combustion in the final act.
>
> Hats off to Director John Lionel Trouper, who has resurrected his career and reputation by skillfully funnelling all of this feminine energy and talent into the best revival of *The Women* that this reviewer has ever seen; certainly, the Best Director nominations will soon be rolling in once again for Mr. Trouper.

John Lionel was, in fact, nominated for yet another Best Director award, and that he accepted the nomination still angers me.

Because our father didn't direct *The Women*.

I did.

And, at least initially, I managed to keep everything under control.

Our father, who was forbidden by our grandmother from interacting directly with any of the actresses, soon became bored with the play after the blocking was finished, and he left most of the coaching and fine-tuning at subsequent rehearsals to me, the assistant director. Since Amber Anderson's character, Edith Phelps Potter, appeared mostly in the first half of the show, and Prudence Petty's Lucy was featured only in the second half, our father would habitually leave the theatre with Prudence when we were rehearsing (and later performing) the play's early scenes, and he would do the same thing with Amber when we were running the later scenes.

This meant that, during Prudence Petty's frequent absences, her daughter, Penny, had to be supervised by whichever other actress happened to be rehearsing or playing a scene with her at the time. Because Penny was cast as Little Mary, the precocious daughter of Mary Haines, the responsibility for Penny's care often fell to Olivia, who shouldered this additional duty without complaint, but with some muted resentment.

Joan's irritation with Prudence Petty's offspring was much less understated. Penny Petty was mature, talented, charming, well-spoken, and perhaps too much like Joan at the same age for her own good. On the rare occasions that John Lionel was present in the theatre, he doted on the little girl, and not only did this drive Joan wild with jealousy, but in the major scene that Penny and Joan played together in the second half of the show, Penny managed to upstage Joan with her wide-eyed-yet-self-aware performance, her Little Mary milking laughs from the audience at the expense of Joan's lead character, Crystal.

As the assistant director and stage manager, I knew I would have to keep Joan as far away as possible from Penny when I overheard this exchange between them, just after they had ducked behind the stage right curtains after playing a pivotal scene together.

"Stop stepping on my lines, you brat," Joan hissed as she grabbed Penny by one of her pigtails.

Penny responded in a precocious tone that resembled a seasoned prima donna much more than a budding child actor, "I'm not stepping on your lines, you brazen ham. You're stepping on mine."

Joan tugged Penny's pigtail again, harder this time. "And stop milking your exit line for laughs. It's my name at the top of the bill, not yours."

"That'll change soon enough," Penny huffed, while tugging her pigtail from Joan's grip.

Joan snarled, "Why, you little ...," and she raised an open hand in Penny's face.

Penny stepped closer. "Go ahead and slap me. I'll cry so hard you'll wind up in jail."

Joan growled, "You little bitch," but she was wise enough to place both hands behind her back at the same time.

Penny stuck her tongue out. "I'm telling my mother you said that. And she'll tell your father. And then you'll be in trouble."

Joan pasted on an expression of mock regret. "Oh, I'm sorry I said that, darling. I take it back. Okay?"

"You'd better."

Joan's eyes narrowed, and her voice dropped to a deadly whisper. "I chose the wrong word, my dear. I didn't mean to call you a bitch. I meant to call you a bastard."

Penny's eyes widened.

Joan's eyes glistened with satisfaction. "Go ask your mommy to explain what that word means, honey. Your mommy knows."

Penny burst into tears, and then Joan turned and sauntered away, a *femme fatale* sway upon her hips.

And that was just one backstage exchange, between a woman and a child; some of the conflicts between the other actresses were even more extreme.

The catfight scene in *The Women* was an audience favourite, and, as tensions escalated, both onstage and off, it got better with every show. Our father's blocking for this scene, like every other sequence in the production, was copied directly from the 1939 movie:

SCENE: A dude ranch in Reno, Nevada, where OLIVIA's character, Mary Haines, has arrived so she can get a "quickie" divorce from her husband (who has been cheating on her with JOAN's Crystal Allen). They meet MARIGOLD's Miriam Aarons and CHRYSANTHEMUM's Countess Flora de Lave, who are also staying at the same ranch for similar reasons.

When VIOLET's character, Sylvia Fowler, arrives at the ranch, fresh from her own divorce, she discovers that MARIGOLD's Miriam is the woman with whom her own husband has been cheating.

Annnnnd... cue the catfight!

VIOLET pulls MARIGOLD from the horse she's been riding (it was a real horse in the film, but our onstage stallion is made from papier-mâché), and MARIGOLD responds by ripping off VIOLET's glasses and slapping her in the face. While the other women try to wrestle them apart, VIOLET pulls MARIGOLD's hair, and MARIGOLD tugs VIOLET's hat down over her face.

After this dramatic prelude, MARIGOLD's Miriam and VIOLET's Sylvia begin seriously scrapping, quite literally kicking each other's asses before rolling around on the ground together in a clawing, swatting, choking wrestling match, during which several articles of clothing are torn and pulled off.

OLIVIA finally drags MARIGOLD off of VIOLET, and CHRYSANTHEMUM sits upon VIOLET to hold her down.

VIOLET still manages to bite MARIGOLD's ankle before OLIVIA finally drags MARIGOLD away.

This scene was met with enthusiastic laughter and cheering from the audience every night, and the actresses fed on the applause, staging the fight faster and more intensely each time. They became so invested in this scene that, by the final week of the show, it teetered on the edge of a real brawl.

For one thing, the blocking for this scene was genuinely dangerous. I tried to coach Marigold to pull her slap as much as possible, but every once in a while, in the heat of her performance, she would land a hard one on Violet's face, which would nearly knock her sideways. This would get Violet's adrenaline up, and she would respond with a particularly spirited hair-pull, often stomping away with some of Marigold's hair clenched in her fists.

By the final week of the show, Marigold's hair was thinner, and her ankle was scabbed over from all the times that Violet's teeth accidentally broke through her skin, and Violet had a thick layer of skin-toned makeup covering the bruise on her left cheek where she had been repeatedly slapped by Marigold.

Olivia and our grandmother took their lumps as well; Olivia lost count of the number of times that she was elbowed in the chest and kicked in the shins when she dragged the thrashing Marigold away from Violet, and even our grandmother absorbed a few blows as she sat on top of Violet's character to restrain her.

The only actress onstage who escaped injury in this scene was Prudence Petty, who, as Lucy, the caretaker of the dude ranch, merely stood in the background offering acerbic commentary on the battle in progress. During our final performance of *The Women*, however, my sisters collectively ensured that Prudence Petty would be added to the injured list in a very decisive way.

As for everything that happened in between, well, here is a concise selection of highlights from my assistant director's notes:

- The traditional sibling rivalry between Violet and Joan is amplified by the unique pressures of this show, and neither ever misses an opportunity to point out when the other has made a mistake, onstage or off. As always, I am careful to avoid taking sides.

- Marigold and Violet's onstage conflict affects their offstage demeanour with each other, and both are twitchy and uneasy in the other's presence; I have to be particularly neutral in this situation because Violet cries, "You're favouring Marigold!" whenever I ask her to ease up, and Marigold exclaims, "You're siding with Violet!" whenever I do the opposite.

- This situation becomes even more complicated when our grandmother chastises Violet and Marigold for the "careless" injuries she sustains while "breaking up the scrap" during the catfight scene.

- All of my sisters take every opportunity to show their disrespect for Amber Anderson and Prudence Petty, who both have participated in extramarital trysts with our father in the past and who both therefore contributed to our mother's breakdown, which caused her exile to the Sunrise Mental Health and Addiction Recovery Colony. I myself am trying to remain civil and professional with them, but it isn't easy.

- The Trouper Sisters are also intentionally cold, distant, and outright malicious to child actress Penny Petty, who appears to be the direct biological result of our father's previous affair with Prudence Petty.

- To make matters worse, in addition to their cold war with the Trouper Sisters, Amber Anderson and Prudence Petty are openly hostile toward each other because both are apparently competing to rekindle old flames with our father.

- Marigold is increasingly angry at our grandmother for funding our mother's incarceration, and she throws shade at Chrysanthemum, in front of the other actresses, at every opportunity. Although she is certainly out of practice after her sixty-year hiatus from the stage, our proud and self-assured grandmother is more than willing to throw it right back at Marigold, and at anyone else who questions her talent or authority.

- Olivia, in turn, is resentful toward everyone else in the bickering cast because she feels that she is carrying the burden of the show's success or failure on her shoulders and that her grades are slipping as a result.

- Violet has similar feelings toward the rest of us because our rehearsals, and now the shows, have cut into her rehearsal time with Kitty Galore, with whom she feels her creative future lies.

- Joan, as always, feels like everyone else is dragging her down and holding her back from the stardom she feels she has already earned.

- And Marigold just ticks away quietly in the background like a time bomb, counting the days until the show will end, until she will turn eighteen and she can sign our mother out of the Sunrise Colony and bring her home again.

When I tried to share these observations with our father, he brushed past me and said flatly, "Not such an easy job after all, is it, big shot?" Then he left the theatre with the giggling Amber Anderson.

AND SO, DURING EVERY night of our run of *The Women*, the stage of the Orpheum-Galaxie became a cauldron that we filled with a dozen volatile elements, stirring them together and heating them to a boil, and we fed our concoction to each consecutive audience, who were hungry for drama and tension and conflict and betrayal, and they ravenously devoured it.

After the opening night show, which received a standing ovation during curtain call, Marigold patted me on the back and said, "George Cukor would be proud of you, Errol."

She knew that I had always been a fan of Cukor's work, and what film buff isn't? Not only was he the director of the film version of *The Women*, which we were more or less reproducing scene for scene onstage, but he directed some of the best films of Hollywood's Golden Age, including some of my personal favourites: *Little Women*, *Dinner at Eight*, *David Copperfield*, *Romeo and Juliet*, *Camille*, *The Philadelphia Story*, *A Woman's Face*, *Gaslight*, *Adam's Rib*, *A Star Is Born*, *Bhowani Junction*, and *My Fair Lady*.

Cukor had built a reputation as a great "women's director" after coaxing award-winning and career-defining performances out of Katharine Hepburn, Ingrid Bergman, Ava Gardner, Marie Dressler, Jean Harlow, Greta Garbo, Judy Garland, and Audrey Hepburn (not to mention the entire cast of *The Women*), and he spent countless hours coaching Vivien Leigh and Olivia de Havilland in their iconic roles in *Gone with the Wind* before he was fired and replaced as the film's director.

Some Hollywood insiders claim that it was Clark Gable who demanded that Cukor be fired from *Gone with the Wind* so he could work with a "man's man" (this despite the fact that Cukor still holds the record for directing the most Academy Award–winning performances in the Best Actor category). Other accounts proclaim that Cukor was fired because his perfectionist tendencies were costing producer David O. Selznick too much money on an already expensive film. Either way, Cukor's fate was in the hands of another more powerful, more headstrong man, a situation that I certainly understood.

Anyway, Cukor's firing from *Gone with the Wind* made him available to direct *The Women*, and the rest is history; he deserves a special award just for managing to keep Joan Crawford and Norma Shearer from killing each other off camera.

Alas, on May 25, 1995, on the day that we Fabulous Trouper Quintuplets turned eighteen, on the evening of our final performance of *The Women*, it became obvious that I was no George Cukor.

The cauldron finally boiled over, and everything burst into flames.

Scene 27:

The Final Scene

(Or: Life Imitating Art)

AFTER THE CURTAINS CLOSED on the evening of our penultimate performance of *The Women*, Marigold wandered up to me backstage and said, "Let's go look at the Falls tonight."

I shrugged. "Why? We see them every day."

"And we shouldn't take them for granted," she said quietly. "After our final show tomorrow, everything is going to change."

I hadn't had time to think about it until then: the next day, the Trouper Quintuplets would all officially be adults, and at least four of us had our eyes on individual futures that would take us far away from the stage upon which we had lived our entire lives.

So, we walked to the Falls, Marigold and I, and we stood together on the observation deck, watching the multicoloured projected lights dancing upon the rush of falling water.

"This is nice," Marigold said, and she placed her hand on my shoulder.

"It is," I said.

Then, at midnight, the lights were switched off, and the Falls went dark.

THE NEXT EVENING, DURING the closing performance of *The Women* at the Trouper-Royale Orpheum-Galaxie Theatre, the final version of the catfight scene played out like this:

SCENE: Onstage at the Orpheum-Galaxie, on the set of the Reno Dude Ranch, a super-adrenalized VIOLET pulls MARIGOLD from the papier mâché horse with so much additional vigor that MARIGOLD goes flying into OLIVIA, knocking her down, and the horse tumbles over onto VIOLET.

VIOLET kicks the inanimate horse away with all the strength in her soccer-toned legs, and it spirals through the air and lands upstage, knocking PRUDENCE PETTY backward into the rear stage scenery, which crashes over in a thundering roar, revealing the backstage cinderblock walls.

In an attempt to get the scene back on the rails, MARIGOLD disentangles herself from OLIVIA and sprints back to her mark downstage. As she rushes away, she accidentally elbows OLIVIA in the chest and knocks the wind out of her, and OLIVIA falls gasping onto the floorboards.

A dazed VIOLET, who was slammed pretty hard by the falling equine prop, rises shakily up onto her feet to be met by a hard, running face-slap from MARIGOLD, who forgets to pull off VIOLET's glasses first, and they fly from her face and out into the audience.

Instead of pulling MARIGOLD's hair (as per the scene's original blocking), VIOLET delivers a full-powered retaliatory roundhouse slap to

MARIGOLD's face with a cracking sound that reverberates through the theatre. Several delighted spectators cheer.

Stunned, MARIGOLD instinctively rushes at VIOLET, and a concussed VIOLET rushes back at her. Their foreheads clunk together, and both women tumble onto the floorboards. VIOLET is knocked out cold, and MARIGOLD hovers on the edge of unconsciousness.

As PRUDENCE PETTY climbs up from atop the collapsed rear stage scenery, though, MARIGOLD shakily rises and ambles over to her.

MARIGOLD TROUPER. This is for my mother.

MARIGOLD shoves PRUDENCE, who crashes down onto the fallen scenery once again. PRUDENCE struggles to get back to her feet with fists clenched and rage in her eyes.

PRUDENCE PETTY. You're going to pay for that, little girl.

JOAN emerges from backstage and stands beside MARIGOLD, raising her fists dramatically.

JOAN TROUPER. (to PRUDENCE PETTY) Think you can take us both? (a dramatic pause) Stay down, Prudence. Stay down.

Wisely, PRUDENCE PETTY stays down. Her daughter, PENNY, runs onto the stage and dives onto her mother's lap.

PENNY PETTY. Mommy! Mommy! Mommy!

PRUDENCE PETTY clutches PENNY against her, using her as a human shield against JOAN and MARIGOLD.

JOAN turns and strides out to centre stage with her fists still raised.

JOAN TROUPER. And where is the other one? Where is Amber Anderson? Come and get yours, too, Amber.

JOAN raises the volume of her voice so it thunders through the auditorium.

JOAN TROUPER. Amber! Amber! Amber!

Soon the crowd is chanting along with JOAN, "AMBER! AMBER! AMBER!"

Backstage, a flabbergasted ERROL reaches up and pulls the rope to close the curtains on the calamity unfolding onstage, but for the first time in the history of the Orpheum-Galaxie Theatre, the mechanism jams, and the curtains stay open.

ERROL tugs again, harder, which pulls loose an overhead counterweight from a well-worn pulley. Concrete dust explodes from the plummeting burlap sack as it pounds the top of JOAN's head, instantly coating her in grey powder. JOAN falls to the stage like a statue of a French queen on Bastille Day.

CHRYSANTHEMUM TROUPER. Oh, dear. Oh, my.

CHRYSANTHEMUM clutches her chest and tumbles onto the stage with the rest of the actresses.

From backstage, ERROL sees the chain reaction of bodies hitting the floorboards, and he immediately sprints through the dark, narrow backstage corridor and then down the cast-iron staircase, his feet ringing on the metal steps.

In the dark, ERROL almost runs right over JOHN LIONEL TROUPER and AMBER ANDERSON, who are locked in an embrace halfway down the spiral staircase. AMBER's dress is pulled up, and JOHN LIONEL's pants are pulled down.

JOHN LIONEL TROUPER. Jeezus, Errol!

AMBER ANDERSON. Shit! Is it curtain call already?

AMBER pulls down her dress, pushes past ERROL, and scampers up the stairs.

JOHN LIONEL TROUPER glares menacingly at ERROL while standing with his pants still down around his ankles.

JOHN LIONEL TROUPER. I swear, if you say anything to my mother or my daughters, I'll —

ERROL TROUPER. Let me by.

JOHN LIONEL blocks ERROL.

JOHN LIONEL TROUPER. You keep your mouth shut. You didn't see anything.

ERROL TROUPER. You fucking asshole! Everyone knows! Who do you think you're fooling?

ERROL shoves JOHN LIONEL, and because JOHN LIONEL's ankles are bound by his dropped pants, he falls backward and thumps down the stairs on his behind, slamming headfirst against the wall at the bottom of the flight. ERROL checks JOHN LIONEL — he has a pulse and he's breathing. Then ERROL steps over his father, runs for the phone in the lobby, and dials 911.

ERROL TROUPER. Send ambulances to the Trouper-Royale Orpheum-Galaxie Theatre on Clifton Hill. (a pause) As many as you've got.

I've heard it said that the easiest way to tell the difference between a Shakespearean drama and one of the Bard's tragedies is to look at the end of Act Three: if the stage is littered with bodies, then the play is a tragedy. By this measure, *The Women* finished its run as a tragedy of truly Shakespearean proportions.

Even as the paramedics carried away the stretchers loaded with moaning, crying, or unconscious actresses, I continued my duties as the show's stage manager. One of the paramedics informed me that the injured would be transported two to an ambulance, and, for everyone's safety, I had a responsibility to ensure that certain casualties didn't end up riding together.

I had to keep Violet and Joan apart for the usual reasons, but Joan also had to be kept away from her latest archrival, Penny Petty, who had emerged from the melee uninjured but who would have to accompany her mother, Prudence, to the hospital; Prudence had suffered a possible concussion when she was hit by the flying *papier mâché* horse, a sprained ankle when she tumbled backward through the scenery, and a bruised tailbone when Marigold shoved her down that second time.

I also had to keep all of my sisters away from Prudence Petty and Amber Anderson. Amber wasn't part of the catfight scene, so she had initially escaped injury, but when she heard the crowd chanting "AMBER! AMBER! AMBER!", she assumed that she was being summoned for the show's final curtain call, and, as she sprinted onto the stage, a dust-caked Joan stuck her leg out and tripped her, causing Amber to break a wrist when she cartwheeled over the debris of the destroyed set.

The last problem was my own: if anyone let me within striking distance of our father, there was the possibility that I might kill him.

When I explained all of this to the lead paramedic, she just grinned and quoted a Humphrey Bogart line from *Casablanca*: "Well, the geography may be difficult to arrange ..."

Everyone made it to the hospital alive, and the emergency room doctor treated each fallen actor in turn. After assuring me that everyone's injuries were much less critical than all the moaning and crying suggested, and that Grandma Trouper's "heart attack" was actually only a mild case of stress-induced acid reflux, she suggested that I should take a walk for the sake of my own mental health.

I immediately went looking for Marigold, who had gone missing in action shortly after the onstage melee.

Marigold would know what to say to put all of this in perspective.

Scene 28:

The Gorge

(Or: Sewn-on Golden Angel Wings)

IT WAS A DESOLATE experience walking from the hospital toward the flickering glow of downtown Niagara Falls in the wee hours of the morning. The curbside parking spots were mostly empty, and there was hardly another person to be seen, except for the occasional drunk staggering back to their hotel. The sodium vapour streetlights hummed ominously overhead, painting the shuttered, lightless buildings on the outskirts of downtown with a surreal amber glow. My footsteps echoed against the sidewalk like slaps in the face.

The sun was rising by the time I'd walked along the river all the way home to Trouper Terrace. As I climbed to the top of the twisting gravel driveway, I saw a police cruiser parked in front of the old carriage house and a uniformed officer standing on the front veranda, knocking on the door.

A shiver bristled the hairs on my skin.

The carriage house was empty. The Renault Floride was gone.

My stomach twisted and my vision blurred as I realized that Marigold had gone to rescue our mother.

Without me. I had forgotten all about it.

I heard Marigold's voice cooing, "After our final show, everything is going to change."

The police officer turned toward me as I approached.

"John Lionel Trouper?"

"No," I said. "I'm Errol." Then I added reluctantly, "John Lionel's son."

In one hand, the police officer held Marigold's backpack, its sewn-on golden angel wings flopping down upon the warped floorboards of the veranda.

"Where did you get that?" I asked.

The lead-eyed officer handed the backpack to me. "Can you identify this?"

"It's my sister Marigold's backpack."

"It was found at the scene," the police officer said.

"The scene of ...?"

He paused and looked down before making eye contact with me again. "I regret to inform you that there has been an accident."

"An accident?"

"About an hour ago, a Renault Floride, registered to one Lily Royale-Trouper —"

"That's my mother."

"I hate that I have to ask you this, son, but ... have you reached the age of majority?"

"I turned eighteen today. Or yesterday, I mean."

The police officer then described, in more detail than I could fully process, the scene that would fuel my nightmares for years to come: the knocked-down guardrail at the top of the cliff, the

Renault Floride smashed almost beyond recognition at the bottom of the river gorge, the forensic evidence that suggested that the bodies of Marigold and our mother had been thrown from the car and into the rushing river.

"Your mother's body washed up just upstream from the crash site," said the sombre officer, "but we'll have to drag the river to retrieve your sister. And with the water moving at such a speed, she's likely already out in the lake by now anyway, so don't get your hopes up."

"Okay," was all I could manage to say.

AFTER THE POLICE CRUISER disappeared down the driveway, leaving behind a thick plume of dust like a rocket's trail, I slung Marigold's angel-winged backpack over my shoulder, and I walked away from Trouper Terrace, along the river, and toward the glow of town.

The Falls roared darkly as I passed; the coloured lights had been switched off many hours earlier.

I walked past the hotels, past the themed restaurants, past the wax museum and the haunted house, past the Trouper-Royale Orpheum-Galaxie Theatre, past the blinking lights and humming neon, past the high school, past the hospital, and toward the highway out of town.

And I kept walking for a long, long time after that.

Scene 29:

The Long Goodbye

(Or: Splinters on the Concrete)

SO NOW HERE WE are, the four surviving members of the Fabulous Trouper Quintuplets, sitting together around the table in the black-and-white tiled kitchen of Trouper Terrace, looking and then not looking at one another, each of us waiting for someone else to deliver the opening line.

Joan sighs, opens her huge sequin-studded purse, and removes a martini glass, an airplane mini-bottle of vodka, and another of dry vermouth. Then she ceremoniously places the glass on the tabletop and simultaneously pours both bottles into it, one from each hand. Finally, she removes a small jar of green olives from inside her purse and drops one into her drink.

"Without olives," she says, "a martini just ..."

She releases a second olive from between two long, red-lacquered fingernails.

"... doesn't ..."

A third olive plops into the glass.

"... cut it."

I recognize that she's paraphrasing one of Elliott Gould's lines from the film *M*A*S*H*, and I send Joan a slight smile of recognition. She doesn't see it, though, or if she does, she doesn't react.

Violet grabs a bottle of beer from the fridge, removes a Swiss Army knife from the front pocket of her jeans, and pops the cap off with its bottle opener, a move reminiscent of the moment she had her first swig of Scallywag Sparky's "Naturally Effervescent" Grape Soda.

Olivia sighs and removes a silver-plated flask from the inside pocket of her jacket, then she plucks a glass from a cabinet and pours herself a generous dram of single malt Scotch.

It looks like I am the only one of us who will face this meeting without the comfort of my favourite drink; a bottle of red wine is difficult to hide inside a suit jacket. Olivia sees my predicament, though, and she removes another glass from the cabinet, pours what's left of her flask into it, and hands it to me.

We all drink in silence until finally Olivia speaks.

"Well, the easiest way to satisfy the conditions of the will," she intones, "would be to just produce a revival of *The Women* with everyone playing the same roles as in our original show."

Joan's eyes bug out. "I said it before, and I'll say it again: There is no way in hell that I am sharing the stage again with Amber Anderson or Prudence Petty ... never mind that demon spawn Penny."

Olivia shrugs and says evenly, "Then there is no way in hell that you will see any money from our father's estate. And neither will any of the rest of us."

Joan crosses her arms and looks away.

"Listen, Joan," Olivia says, maintaining her businesslike tone. "Since you're the one with the most acting credits, your name will go at the top of the bill."

Joan smoulders petulantly for a moment, biting her bottom lip before finally huffing, "Fine. But don't expect me to be *nice*."

Violet mumbles, "Just be yourself."

To prevent another battle between Joan and Violet, Olivia immediately continues. "So, then, Joan will reprise her role as Crystal Allen, Violet will play Sylvia Fowler, I'll play Mary Haines, Errol will direct, and we can —"

"Hold on," Violet interrupts. "I can't do it. Kitty Galore has gigs booked. I can't leave my ladies in the lurch."

As a development executive at AMUSEMENT ELEVEN™, Olivia is used to thinking quickly in negotiations. "What if," she says to Violet, "we allocated some money from the production budget to hire Kitty Galore to play as the pit band for the show?"

Joan scoffs. "What production budget?"

Olivia narrows her eyes at Joan. "Leave that to me. I've got a few executive producers who owe me favours. It'll be enough." She turns back to Violet. "And I like this idea. Having your band play as part of the show might add a contemporary dimension to what is admittedly a dated script, and maybe attract a younger demographic to the theatre."

Joan looks dubiously at Olivia. "Seriously? Daddy would never —"

"'Daddy' isn't producing this show," Olivia says. "I am."

Joan rolls her eyes and huffs dramatically, but she says nothing.

Violet beams. "Hell, yeah! I'll head back to the theatre and tell the ladies right now."

"Your band came to the funeral?" Joan scoffs.

"Of course they did. They're my sisters," Violet says to her actual sister, and her chains and buckles jangle as she rises from the table and strides out of the kitchen.

Joan also stands, her chin raised high, and she says regally,

"Well, I've got fans waiting for me back at the theatre, and they'll be expecting me to put in an appearance." She glides over the tiled floor as if she's walking the red carpet at an awards ceremony. "Call me when rehearsals begin."

Olivia downs the rest of her Scotch, sets down the glass, and rises from her seat.

"Okay," she says, "let's go, Errol."

"Let's go where?"

"Downstairs to the basement."

"Umm ... why?"

"To scour our father's office for a more recent version of his will. Or anything else that will get us out of this mess."

AS I DESCEND WITH Olivia into the basement of Trouper Terrace for the first time in more than two decades, my mind is flooded with dark memories. As we tromp down the creaky steps, my heart palpitates and I feel light-headed. When my feet touch the concrete floor at the bottom of the staircase, a shiver runs up through my body; although I spent a disproportionate part of my childhood down here, I can't help feeling like I'm about to step into Room 237 at the Overlook Hotel in *The Shining*.

Olivia turns toward our father's office and exclaims, "Oh my gawd!"

The door hangs open on half-broken hinges, surrounded by splinters of wood scattered across the concrete, reminding me of the shredded bits of photographs that our mother hurled down onto this same floor so many years ago.

Olivia and I hesitate for a moment outside the Great John Lionel Trouper's sacred sanctuary; none of us have been inside this room since our father had the lock installed so many years ago. Then we step inside.

Olivia flicks a switch, and several Tiffany-style chandeliers ignite overhead, casting dim, coloured light upon the papers, folders, photographs, and award statuettes strewn across the parquet floor. All of the drawers are open on the massive inlaid cherrywood desk, and the glass doors on the display cases have been opened or smashed. The gold-framed *Grand Hotel* poster that hung above our father's desk has been taken down from the wall, and it lies broken on the floor.

"It doesn't look like anything of value has been taken," Olivia notes as she tiptoes over the wreckage, "so it wasn't a robbery." She rifles through the half-emptied contents of a jimmied-open file cabinet drawer. "Someone was looking for something ... but what?" She moves on to our father's gleaming cherrywood desk, which is covered in scattered documents and other debris. She reaches into one of the open desk drawers and removes a chrome-plated revolver, then winks at me, spins around dramatically, and aims the gun at one of trophy cases. She closes one eye and points the barrel at each of our father's prizes: a board game and comic books featuring *The Scallywags*, a soup can and a box of soap flakes featuring John Lionel as a cherubic child actor, the obsessively polished Best Actor and Best Director trophies, the framed photos of our father posing onstage with various young, beautiful female co-stars.

"Wait! Don't! It's not like in the movies. The bullet could ricochet or —"

"Chill out, Errol. It's just a prop from one of his plays." She sighs and lowers the fake gun. "Putting bullet holes in this stuff would have been very, very satisfying, though."

I nod. I understand.

Olivia glances back through the shattered doorframe and across the basement at our rehearsal stage, which, in contrast to our father's lacquered oak-panelled office space, was slapped together from rough-hewn lumber and topped with inexpensive plywood from which the soles of our feet absorbed countless splinters.

Still playing the film noir detective to maximum effect, Olivia raises her nose in the air, sniffs, and says, "Do you smell smoke, or am I just having an aneurysm?"

Olivia follows her nose to the office doorway, and I follow her. In the dim light of the basement, I smell the smoke before I see it, rising from the rehearsal stage in hazy ringlets.

Then I see the slender, black-clad figure again, sprinting from the stage toward the staircase, face obscured by a black sweatshirt hood, a file folder gripped in one black-gloved hand.

At the other end of the basement, the rehearsal stage bursts into flames.

In a flurry of footsteps, the dark figure disappears up the stairs.

Olivia yelps, "Run!"

We run, chasing the thieving arsonist up the stairs, through the foyer of Trouper Terrace, the dining room, the kitchen, and out through the back door. Olivia and I emerge outside to see the dark figure sprinting through the overgrown backyard of Trouper Terrace toward the thick forest on the other side of the fallen wire fence.

"Stop!" Olivia hollers, pointing the prop pistol at the escaping figure's back. "Drop what you've stolen, or I'll shoot you dead!"

The black-clad interloper drops the file folder in the tall grass, but she keeps running; despite her baggy, androgynous black clothing, despite the hood and scarf that obscure her face, I am pretty sure now that our invader is female.

Olivia drops to her knees, grabs the discarded file folder, and removes a document from inside. "It's an insurance policy!" she calls out to me.

I keep running in pursuit of the shadowy trespasser, not because she broke in to our childhood home, not because she seems to have stolen an insurance document from our father's office, not because she has apparently set our rehearsal stage on fire, but because I now suspect that she isn't really a trespasser at all.

The dim, diffused light of this cloudy afternoon causes the design on the back of her hoodie to momentarily shine: in nearly invisible black applique, the escaping arsonist thief wears a stylized pair of angel's wings.

Scene 30:

The Phantom

(Or: Free Yourselves)

"HEY!" I CALL OUT to her. "Wait! Stop!"

But she keeps running, leaping over the sagging wires of the dilapidated backyard fence and sprinting into the thick, dark woods beyond. By the time I cross the property line myself, she has vanished once again.

I stop and squint through the shadowy spaces between the trees and scrub, but it's no use. In her all-black outfit, I will never see her.

But then, in the distance, muffled by the foliage and almost buried beneath the roar of the river at the bottom of the slope, I hear a screech.

I recognize that sound. It's the hinges on the door of the Honeycomb Hideout.

Leaves and twigs snap under my feet as I start running again, and as I scramble down the hill, I see it. The decrepit old cabin is leaning even further toward the river now, and almost all of the yellowed white paint has flaked away, the brown-stained wood underneath rotting through and crumbling. Weeds and saplings sprout from the roof and eaves.

When I step into the musty shack, though, there is no one inside, but there is a message scrawled upon a peeling bit of old wallpaper still stuck to the crumbling, mould-covered wall.

Free yourselves

When I try to peel the scrap of wallpaper away, it crumbles and disintegrates.

I run outside the Honeycomb Hideout, my senses supercharged, but all I hear is the Niagara River rushing at the bottom of the slope and fire roaring at the top, and all I see are tendrils of smoke creeping downhill through the trees.

I watch and listen for what seems like a long time, but there is nothing. She is gone.

As I finally climb the hill toward Trouper Terrace, the lingering scent of mould and decay from the Honeycomb Hideout is replaced by a smell like burning toast and smoking tires.

All I feel as I trudge uphill are a few brittle scraps of wallpaper stuck to my thumb and index finger.

When I step over the fence, I see Violet and Joan running from the opposite direction.

"What the hell?" Violet gasps, to which Joan breathlessly adds, "We turned back as soon as we saw the smoke."

Olivia joins us, still gripping the insurance policy in one hand, and my sisters and I stand together at the edge of the property, watching with wide eyes as Trouper Terrace goes up in flames like a late-autumn brush pile.

We observe as the family of itinerant raccoons — five of them all together — flee from underneath the wraparound veranda as it bursts into roaring flames.

As the inferno climbs the dilapidated mansion's tallest Italianate tower, Olivia puts her arm around my waist and pulls me close. As flaming tiles fly from the engulfed Mansard roof like projectiles from an erupting volcano, Violet also puts an arm around me.

The fireballs pummel the roof of the nearby carriage house, and it also bursts into flames, then the central tower collapses, exploding on the ground in a roaring cloud of fire and smoke and ash.

Joan cries, "Oh!" as she throws both of her arms around Violet and presses her tear-slicked face against her sister's shoulder.

We hear the sirens approaching, but it is already too late. Before the first fire truck arrives, Trouper Terrace will have been devoured from the inside. Its hollowed shell will collapse in upon itself, and soon nothing will remain but a foundation full of rubble and ash.

And Olivia, Violet, Joan, and I will stand together and cling to one another as our childhood home vanishes before our eyes, its glowing embers blinking out as they rise upward, its smoke rising upward like a phantom, disappearing into the inky sky.

Scene 31:

The Phoenix Effect

(Or: Buy a Ticket)

SO, IT WOULD APPEAR that Marigold made a choice.

It would appear that she survived.

It would appear that she escaped.

It would appear that she created another life for herself and that she returned to potentially provide the rest of us with the same opportunity.

Maybe she also returned to make sure that our father really was finally gone.

Or maybe it wasn't Marigold at all.

Maybe I just imagined the stylized angel wings on her back.

Maybe the message inside the Honeycomb Hideout was left by someone else for someone else.

Maybe it was just another arsonist thief who randomly grabbed a forgotten fire insurance policy that would pay out to John Lionel Trouper's next of kin ... there was also some cash and bearer bonds in the folder.

Either way, Marigold is no longer with us. And, as terribly as I miss her, I don't think she is ever coming back.

But for Joan, Violet, Olivia, and I, the questions remain.

Can any of us ever really change in any substantive way?

How much can a coin vary from the die from which it has been struck?

How much can a sculpture grow from the confines of the mould into which its material was poured and hardened?

These questions fill my head as I sit in a front-row seat in the sold-out auditorium of the Royale Orpheum-Galaxie Theatre, waiting for the curtain to open on the premiere performance of our show *The Phoenix Effect*.

Yes, we decided to keep the theatre.

And yes, we removed our father's name from the marquee. We removed his name from ourselves, too; we are now known as the Royale Quintuplets: Errol, Olivia, Violet, and Joan Royale. We all believe that our late mother would have appreciated this gesture and everything that it means.

And, yes, the decision was unanimous; even Joan eventually agreed to the change, maybe because the spell that our father cast upon her gradually dissolved as his influence became more distant, maybe because she grew closer to her siblings when she no longer had to compete for our father's approval and affection ... and maybe also because she loved the regal, destined-for-greatness sound of the name *Joan Royale*.

And yes, our first show without our father really is sold out. The viral videos from the funeral certainly gave us some free publicity, and the widely reported investigation into the arson at Trouper Terrace didn't hurt either (and, thanks to the many fans of Joan and Violet who testified that none of the Trouper siblings ever left the theatre that day, none of us were ever even suspects).

And yes, we're doing a show of our own. We're not reviving *The Women*. We didn't call Amber Anderson or Prudence or Penny Petty. We didn't have to, because the lawyer accidentally left the cassette tape, the only copy of John Lionel Trouper's last will and testament, inside the tape player that is now melted and scorched and buried beneath the ashes of Trouper Terrace. We never heard from her again, even after the cheques and the deeds were delivered.

As I wait with the rest of the capacity crowd for the show to begin, I am at peace with all of it, yet those old nagging questions continue to fill my mind.

Once a performer has been typecast, are they ever really believable in any other kind of role? To the public, to other performers, to themselves?

Joan is the only one of us who will be onstage when the curtains open for the premiere of *The Phoenix Effect*. She will be playing all five of the quintuplets; in this version of the story, they are identical.

Can she pull it off? Can she play five different characters with different personalities, strengths, flaws, talents, desires, motivations?

Well, Joan has the talent. She's always had it. She loves the stage, and the stage loves her.

I wrote the script, and I directed the play.

How did I do it? How did I create a story in which one actor plays five different roles on the same stage? Mirrors? Projections? Special effects? Body doubles? (Body triplets… quadruplets?)

Well, it turns out that I'm a good director. I always have been. It just took me some time to realize it.

Olivia is the producer. She also cast the show.

And how could she afford to mount such a daring production?

How did she assemble such a famous, all-star cast? Where did she find such an exceptional tech crew?

Well, Olivia is organized, hardworking, and self-disciplined. She's a born producer. She always has been.

From the newly built band pit at the front of the stage, high-voltage energy crackles like nothing ever heard before inside the Orpheum-Galaxie as Kitty Galore flawlessly plays an aggressive, up-tempo, distorted-electric-guitar version of "Sisters Are Doin' It for Themselves"; when Violet begins belting out the lyrics, everyone in the sold-out house cheers like they're at a stadium rock concert.

But can this story work as a musical? Will this show — as pitched by Olivia to the investors — be *Tommy* meets *Waiting for Guffman* meets *The Royal Tenenbaums*? Will it all come together?

Well, Violet is a rock star. She always has been.

In this version of the story, will the Prodigal Daughter return?

Will the Imprisoned Mother triumphantly escape?

Will the Narcissistic Father receive his comeuppance?

And as the music stops and the cheering fades to silence, as the gilt-edged curtains slowly open on *The Phoenix Effect*, the lingering question still remains.

Can any of us — Joan, Violet, Olivia, me — can any one of us ever become anything other than what our father raised us to be?

Maybe the answer is yes.

Maybe the answer is no.

Maybe the answer is maybe.

Maybe the answer is sometimes.

But each one of us, in our own way, is trying to find out.

And maybe that's enough.

But come and see for yourself. Buy a ticket for the show.

Scene 32:
The Daydream
(Or: Go Forward)

AND HERE I AM dreaming again.

Everything is vivid, vintage Technicolor, all primary and secondary tones, as if coloured with a pack of grade-school crayons. The sky is Pacific Blue, and the paper-white clouds overhead are traced in Sunset Orange.

I'm driving a speeding convertible. It is Basic Black.

In a sudden jump cut, the guardrail that divides the road from the Niagara River gorge appears upon the movie screen of the roaring car's windshield.

I grip the steering wheel in both hands, and I stomp down on the accelerator pedal.

Upon the empty passenger seat beside me, the pages of a magazine riffle in the wind. It's an issue of *Applause* magazine, and upon its cover is a colour photo of Joan, Violet, and Olivia. They have their arms around one another's shoulders, and they are smiling brightly. The title above them reads: "THE ROYALE RENAISSANCE: Sisters Are Doin' It for Themselves."

The wind funnelling into the open cockpit of the convertible snatches the magazine and flings it into the air. In the rearview mirror, I watch it hit the road behind me and flutter for a moment ... then it transforms into a mythical black bird that spreads its wings and rises into the heat-distorted air.

I turn my attention to the road ahead of me, and I brace myself for what's coming.

I grip the steering wheel in my left hand, and I downshift with my right.

As the dark-feathered phoenix soars above me, it cries out in a familiar voice, "You can't go forward until you go back."

The engine roars and the tires squeal as I race through the turn.

I glance up again at the rearview mirror to see the cliffside guardrail disappearing behind me. Then Trouper Terrace, then the Orpheum-Galaxie, and then the rainbow of colours projected upon Niagara Falls vanish, too.

The graceful black bird circles above me, and I almost feel as if I can fly, too.

Then the beautiful bird's feathers turn gold, and she dives over the guardrail, disappearing down into the gorge.

I smile. Although I can no longer see her, I know that she is going to rise again on a warm current of air that will take her far away from this place.

And then the soundtrack music swells, a glorious burst of strings and tympani, and for the first time I feel it, for the first time I know for sure:

I am no longer just a bit player in someone else's story; I'm the star of my own show.

I am the unflappable, stone-faced Buster Keaton, about to take control of the train in *The General*.

I am the brazen, cocky Harrison Ford, about to blast through space at the helm of the *Millennium Falcon* in *Star Wars*.

I am the smooth, confident Humphrey Bogart, about to solve the crime in *The Big Sleep*.

I am the elegant, sophisticated Cary Grant, about to rendezvous with Ingrid Bergman in *Notorious*.

I am cool, capable Steve McQueen, about to stomp on the accelerator to begin the chase scene in *Bullitt*.

I am Errol Trouper, and I am about to write the script for the next chapter in my own adventure.

Filmography

THIS IS A SELECTED list of the films mentioned in *The Troupers*. Although John Lionel Trouper might disapprove of some, the author of this book recommends seeing all of the following movies:

The Tramp (1915). Written, directed by, and starring Charles Chaplin.
The Gold Rush (1925). Written, directed by, and starring Charles Chaplin. NOTE: *The Kid* (1921), *City Lights* (1931), *Modern Times* (1936), and *The Great Dictator* (1940) are also essential Chaplin films.
Derby Day (1925). Directed by Robert McGowan. Starring Our Gang (aka the Little Rascals). Written and produced by Hal Roach.
Don Juan (1926). Directed by Alan Crosland. Starring John Barrymore, Estelle Taylor, and Mary Astor. Based on Lord Byron's epic poem.
The General (1926). Directed by and starring Buster Keaton.
College (1927). Directed by and starring Buster Keaton. NOTE: *Sherlock, Jr.* (1924), *The Cameraman* (1928), and *Steamboat Bill, Jr.* (1928) are also essential Buster Keaton films.
Grand Hotel (1932). Directed by Edmund Goulding. Starring Greta Garbo, John Barrymore, Lionel Barrymore, Wallace Beery, and Joan Crawford. Written by William A. Drake.
Little Women (1933). Directed by George Cukor. Starring Katharine

Hepburn, Joan Bennett, Frances Dee, and Jean Parker. Based on the novel by Louisa May Alcott.

Dinner at Eight (1933). Directed by George Cukor. Starring Jean Dressler, John Barrymore, Jean Harlow, Wallace Beery, and Lionel Barrymore. Adapted from the stage play by Sam B. Harris.

A Midsummer Night's Dream (1935). Directed by Max Reinhardt. Starring Dick Powell and Olivia de Havilland. Based on the play by William Shakespeare.

David Copperfield (1935). Directed by George Cukor. Starring W.C. Fields, Lionel Barrymore, and Maureen O'Sullivan. Based on the novel by Charles Dickens.

Beginner's Luck (1935). Directed by Gus Meins. Starring Our Gang (aka the Little Rascals). Produced by Hal Roach.

Captain Blood (1935). Directed by Michael Curtiz. Starring Errol Flynn, Olivia de Havilland, Basil Rathbone, and Ross Alexander. Based on the novel by Rafael Sabatini.

Romeo and Juliet (1936). Directed by George Cukor. Starring Norma Shearer, Leslie Howard, and John Barrymore. Based on the play by William Shakespeare.

Camille (1936). Directed by George Cukor. Starring Greta Garbo, Robert Taylor, and Lionel Barrymore. Based on the 1848 novel *La Dame aux Camélias* by Alexandre Dumas.

Gone with the Wind (1939). Directed by Victor Fleming (replacing George Cukor). Starring Vivian Leigh, Clark Gable, Olivia de Havilland, and Leslie Howard. Based on the novel by Margaret Mitchell.

The Wizard of Oz (1939). Starring Judy Garland, Ray Bolger, Jack Haley, Bert Lahr, Frank Morgan, Billie Burke, and Margaret Hamilton. Directed by Victor Fleming, Mervyn LeRoy, King Vidor, George Cukor, and Norman Taurog. Based on the novel by L. Frank Baum.

The Women (1939). Directed by George Cukor. Starring Norma Shearer, Joan Crawford, Rosalind Russell, Mary Boland, Paulette Goddard, and Virginia Weidler. Based on the play by Clare Boothe Luce.

The Little Princess (1939). Directed by Walter Lang. Starring Shirley Temple, Richard Greene, Anita Louise, Ian Hunter, Arthur Treacher, and Cesar Romero. Based on the novel *A Little Princess* by Frances Hodgson Burnett.

Dark Victory (1939). Directed by Edmund Goulding. Starring Bette

Davis, Humphrey Bogart, and George Brent. Based on the play by George Brewer and Bertram Bloch.

(NOTE: Yes, 1939 was a pretty epic year for Hollywood movies.)

Waterloo Bridge (1941). Directed by Mervyn LeRoy. Starring Vivien Leigh and Robert Taylor. Based on the play by Robert E. Sherwood.

The Maltese Falcon (1941). Directed by John Huston. Starring Humphrey Bogart, Mary Astor, Peter Lorre, and Sydney Greenstreet. Directed by John Huston. Based on the novel by Dashiell Hammett.

The Lady Eve (1941). Directed by Preston Sturges. Starring Barbara Stanwyck and Henry Fonda. Based on a story by Monckton Hoffe.

The Philadelphia Story (1941). Directed by George Cukor. Starring Katharine Hepburn, Cary Grant, and Jimmy Stewart. Based on the play by Philip Barry.

A Woman's Face (1941). Directed by George Cukor. Starring Joan Crawford, Melvyn Douglas, and Conrad Veidt. Based on the play *Il Était Une Fois* by Francis de Croisset.

Casablanca (1942). Starring Humphrey Bogart, Ingrid Bergman, Paul Henreid, Claude Rains, Sydney Greenstreet, and Peter Lorre. Directed by Michael Curtiz. Based on Murray Burnett and Joan Alison's stage play *Everybody Comes to Rick's*.

Now, Voyager (1942). Directed by Irving Rapper. Starring Bette Davis and Paul Henreid. Based on the novel by Olive Higgins Prouty.

Gaslight (1944). Directed by George Cukor. Starring Ingrid Bergman, Charles Boyer, and Joseph Cotton. Based on the play by Patrick Hamilton.

National Velvet (1944). Directed by Clarence Brown. Starring Elizabeth Taylor, Mickey Rooney, and Donald Crisp. Based on the novel by Enid Bagnold.

Spellbound (1945). Directed by Alfred Hitchcock. Starring Ingrid Bergman and Gregory Peck. Adapted from the novel *The House of Dr. Edwardes* by Hilary Saint George Saunders and John Palmer.

Mildred Pierce (1945). Directed by Michael Curtiz. Starring Joan Crawford. Based on the novel by James M. McCain.

Notorious (1946). Directed by Alfred Hitchcock. Starring Cary Grant, Ingrid Bergman, and Claude Rains. Written by Ben Hecht.

The Big Sleep (1946). Directed by Howard Hawks. Starring Humphrey Bogart, Lauren Bacall, John Ridgely, and Martha Vickers. Based on the novel by Raymond Chandler.

Humoresque (1946). Directed by Jean Negulesco. Starring Joan Crawford and John Garfield. Based on the novel by Fanny Hurst.

Little Women (1949). Directed by Mervyn LeRoy. Starring Janet Leigh, June Allyson, Margaret O'Brien, and Elizabeth Taylor. Based on the novel by Louisa May Alcott.

Adam's Rib (1949). Directed by George Cukor. Starring Spencer Tracy and Katharine Hepburn. Written by Ruth Gordon and Garson Kanin.

Twelve O'Clock High (1949). Directed by Henry King. Starring Gregory Peck, Gary Merrill, Hugh Marlowe, and Dean Jagger. Based on the novel by Sy Bartlett and Beirne Lay Jr.

Sunset Boulevard (1950). Directed and co-written by Billy Wilder. Produced and co-written by Charles Brackett. Starring William Holden, Gloria Swanson, and Erich von Stroheim (with cameos by Cecil B. DeMille, Hedda Hopper, Buster Keaton, H.B. Warner, and Anna Q. Nilsson).

Cyrano de Bergerac (1950). Directed by Michael Gordon. Starring Jose Ferrer and Mala Powers. Based on the play by Edmond Rostand.

A Christmas Carol (1951). Directed by Brian Desmond Hurst. Starring Alastair Sim, Jack Warner, and Kathleen Harrison. Based on the story by Charles Dickens.

Pandora and the Flying Dutchman (1951). Directed by Albert Lewin. Starring Ava Gardner and James Mason. Written by Joe Kaufmann.

Singin' in the Rain (1952). Directed by Stanley Donen and Gene Kelly. Starring Gene Kelly, Debbie Reynolds, and Donald O'Connor. Written by Betty Comden and Adolph Green.

House of Wax (1953). Directed by Andre DeToth. Starring Vincent Price. Based on the story "The Wax Works" by Charles Belden.

La Strada (1954). Directed by Federico Fellini. Starring Anthony Quinn, Guilietta Masina, and Richard Basehart. Written by Federico Fellini, Tullio Pinelli, and Ennio Flaiano.

A Star Is Born (1954). Directed by George Cukor. Starring Judy Garland and James Mason. Written by Moss Hart.

Blackboard Jungle (1955). Written and directed by Richard Brooks. Starring Glen Ford, Sidney Poitier, Vic Morrow, Ann Francis, and Margaret Hayes.

Bhowani Junction (1956). Directed by George Cukor. Starring Ava Gardner and Stewart Ganger. Based on the novel by John Masters.

Cat on a Hot Tin Roof (1958). Directed by Richard Brooks. Starring Elizabeth Taylor and Paul Newman. Based on the play by Tennessee Williams.

Vertigo (1958). Directed by Alfred Hitchcock. Starring James Stewart and Kim Novak. Based on the 1954 novel *D'entre les Morts* by Boileau-Narcejac.

North by Northwest (1959). Directed by Alfred Hitchcock. Starring Cary Grant, James Mason, Eva Marie Saint, and Martin Landau. Screenplay by Ernest Lehman.

Charade (1963). Directed by Stanley Donen. Starring Cary Grant and Audrey Hepburn. Written by Peter Stone and Marc Behm.

My Fair Lady (1964). Directed by George Cukor. Starring Audrey Hepburn and Rex Harrison. Based on the play *Pygmalion* by George Bernard Shaw.

The Sound of Music (1965). Directed by Robert Wise. Starring Julie Andrews and Christopher Plummer. Based on the Rogers and Hammerstein musical of the same name.

2001*: A Space Odyssey* (1968). Directed by Stanley Kubrick. Starring Keir Dullea, Gary Lockwood, William Sylvester, and Douglas Rain. Based on the novel by Arthur C. Clarke.

Bullitt (1968). Directed by Peter Yates. Starring Steve McQueen, Jacqueline Bisset, Robert Vaughn, and Don Gordon. Based on the novel *Mute Witness* by Robert L. Fish.

*M*A*S*H* (1970). Directed by Robert Altman. Starring Donald Sutherland, Elliott Gould, Tom Skerritt, Sally Kellerman, Robert Duvall, Roger Bowen, and René Auberjonois. Screenplay by Ring Lardner Jr. Based on the novel by Richard Hooker.

The Long Goodbye (1973). Directed by Robert Altman. Starring Elliot Gould, Sterling Hayden, Nina van Pallandt, Jim Bouton, and Mark Rydell. Based on the novel by Raymond Chandler.

Tommy (1975). Directed, produced, and written by Ken Russel. Starring Ann-Margret, Oliver Reed, Roger Daltrey, Elton John, Eric Clapton, John Entwistle, Keith Moon, Paul Nicholas, Jack Nicholson, Robert Powell, Arthur Brown, Pete Townshend, and Tina Turner. Based on the album by The Who.

Star Wars (1977). Written and directed by George Lucas. Starring Mark Hamill, Harrison Ford, Carrie Fisher, Peter Cushing, Alec Guinness,

David Prowse, James Earl Jones, Anthony Daniels, Kenny Baker, and Peter Mayhew.

The Shining (1980). Directed by Stanley Kubrick. Starring Jack Nicholson, Shelley Duvall, and Danny Lloyd. Based on the novel by Stephen King.

The Empire Strikes Back (1980). Written by Lawrence Kasdan and George Lucas. Directed by Irving Kershner. Starring Mark Hamill, Harrison Ford, Carrie Fisher, Billy Dee Williams, Anthony Daniels, David Prowse, Kenny Baker, Peter Mayhew, and Frank Oz.

Blade Runner (1982). Directed by Ridley Scott. Starring Harrison Ford, Rutger Hauer, Sean Young, and Edward James Olmos. Adapted from the novel *Do Androids Dream of Electric Sheep?* by Philip K. Dick.

Unknown Chaplin (1983). Documentary about the life and films of Charlie Chaplin. Written and produced by Kevin Brownlow and David Gill. Narrated by James Mason.

Return of the Jedi (1983). Written by Lawrence Kasdan and George Lucas. Directed by Richard Marquand. Starring Mark Hamill, Harrison Ford, Carrie Fisher, Billy Dee Williams, Anthony Daniels, David Prowse, Kenny Baker, Peter Mayhew, and Frank Oz.

The Color Purple (1985). Directed by Steven Spielberg. Starring Margaret Avery, Rae Dawn Chong, Whoopi Goldberg, Danny Glover, and Adolph Caesar. Music by Quincy Jones. Based on the novel by Alice Walker.

Stand by Me (1986). Directed by Rob Reiner. Starring Wil Wheaton, River Phoenix, Corey Feldman, Jerry O'Connell, and Kiefer Sutherland. Based on the story "The Body" by Stephen King.

Ferris Bueller's Day Off (1986). Written, directed, and produced by John Hughes. Starring Matthew Broderick, Alan Ruck, and Mia Sara.

Buster Keaton: A Hard Act to Follow (1987). Documentary about the life and films of Buster Keaton. Written and produced by Kevin Brownlow and David Gill.

The Princess Bride (1987). Directed and produced by Rob Reiner. Screenplay by William Goldman, based on his novel. Starring Cary Elwes, Robin Wright, Mandy Patinkin, Chris Sarandon, Christopher Guest, Wallace Shawn, André the Giant, Peter Falk, Fred Savage, Billy Crystal, and Carol Kane. Music by Mark Knopfler.

Waiting for Guffman (1996). Directed by Christopher Guest. Starring Christopher Guest, Eugene Levy, Catherine O'Hara, Fred Willard, and Parker Posey. Written by Christopher Guest and Eugene Levy.

The Royal Tenenbaums (2001). Directed by Wes Anderson. Starring Gene Hackman, Anjelica Huston, Bill Murray, Gwyneth Paltrow, Ben Stiller, Danny Glover, Luke Wilson, and Owen Wilson. Written by Wes Anderson and Owen Wilson.

Gratitude

FIRST, I OWE A huge debt of gratitude to editor extraordinaire Barry Jowett, whose wise and thoughtful guidance really helped this book become what it was meant to be. Thank you, Barry, you're the best!

Thanks also to Marc Côté, Sarah Cooper, and everyone else at Cormorant for your friendship and your continued faith in me and my stories.

My thanks also to Sam Hiyate, Kelvin Kong, and Terri Brunsting, who all provided me with useful early guidance while this story was still finding its way.

Thank you, Andrea Waters, for your thorough and professional copy editing!

For generous support during the creation of this book, my sincere thanks to the Ontario Arts Council.

As always, thanks to my fun, literate, and loyal friends. To paraphrase Bill Murray, "Be careful who you choose as your friends. I'd rather have four quarters than a hundred pennies." My pockets are full of silver dollars, and I am always grateful.

For their abundant love, support, and encouragement, my thanks as always to my wonderful family, especially my parents, Mike and Judy Scarsbrook.

And, as always, this book is for Danielle, my love, my muse, my best friend, and also for my daughter, Vivienne, the smartest, kindest, bravest girl ever!

Finally, if you just finished reading this book, or if you're about to start, well, I love and appreciate you, too.

We acknowledge the sacred land on which Cormorant Books operates. It has been a site of human activity for 15,000 years. This land is the territory of the Huron-Wendat and Petun First Nations, the Seneca, and most recently, the Mississaugas of the Credit River. The territory was the subject of the Dish With One Spoon Wampum Belt Covenant, an agreement between the Iroquois Confederacy and Confederacy of the Anishinaabe and allied nations to peaceably share and steward the resources around the Great Lakes. Today, the meeting place of Toronto is still home to many Indigenous people from across Turtle Island. We are grateful to have the opportunity to work in the community, on this territory.

We are also mindful of broken covenants and the need to strive to make right with all our relations.